PROSPERO'S ISLAND

Navigating Pastoral Care

Roger Grainger

2010

Order this book online at www.trafford.com
or email orders@trafford.com

Most Trafford titles are also available at major online book retailers.

Printed in Victoria, BC, Canada.

ISBN: 978-1-4269-2927-4 (sc)

*Our mission is to efficiently provide the world's finest, most comprehensive book publishing
service, enabling every author to experience success. To find out how to publish your book, your
way, and have it available worldwide, visit us online at www.trafford.com*

Trafford rev. 4/5/2010

 www.trafford.com

North America & international
toll-free: 1 888 232 4444 (USA & Canada)
phone: 250 383 6864 ♦ fax: 812 355 4082

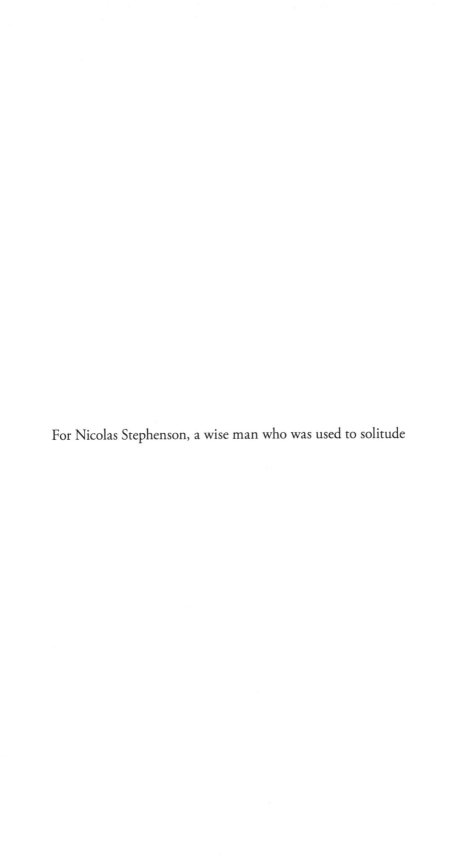

For Nicolas Stephenson, a wise man who was used to solitude

CONTENTS

INTRODUCTION

What has an island to do with pastoral care? More specifically, why choose islands as examples of caring? Do people who live on islands care more for one another than people who live in other places etc? Is there something about islands, or about living on them which contribute to the quality of concern which human beings have for one another. Pastoral care has been defined as "that aspect of the ministry of the Church which is concerned with the well-being of individuals and of communities" (Alistair Campbell A Directory of Pastoral Care)

Nowadays, Campbell's definition seems a little too precise and official; Christians have begun to think of their caring vocation in a less formal and institutional way. On an island, for example, folk are thrown together in close proximity and everybody's priority is sharing rather than any kind of discrimination, even a well meant Christian one. Christians do always represent their faith, but on an island their main credential will be their non-specific human-ness, the awareness particularly marked on such circumstance of 'all being in this together'. The same is likely to be true of members of other religions. Islands throw us together both physically and spiritually and concentrate our awareness of one another's presence. It is more important therefore to develop an awareness of how other people are feeling and what may be concerning them. In these circumstances empathy may be considered a matter of common sense as well as a virtue. Islands concentrate the mind as well as defining the landscape: they manage not to overlap other times and places in the way the mainland does. Surrounded by sea, they turn our gaze on ourselves, other people and the natural world. On an island our awareness of who, what and where we are comes home to us very forcibly – and can hardly be escaped: here 'bearing one another's burdens' is revealed to us as a requirement for survival. Islands are settings for realized metaphor, embodied poetry.

So – Prospero's island "Though this island seem to be desert – Uninhabitable, and almost inaccessible – it must be of subtle, tender and delicate temperance". These are Adrian's words on setting foot on the island where he and the rest of King Alonso's household are shipwrecked. Although seeming deserted it is from the beginning a place waiting to be inhabited; which is why it repeatedly crops up in the chapters which follow where it plays the role of catalyst in a process of exploration and discovery leading to self knowledge – the role which Prospero intended it should have. The argument behind this book is that islands remind us of various kinds of human need and our own role in working for their relief. Pastoral care which is truly other-centred may 'be an island in a sea of troubles'.

DRAMATIS PERSONAE

Alonso, King of Naples

Sebastian, his brother

Prospero, the rightful Duke of Milan

Antonio, his brother, the usurping Duke of Milan

Ferdinand, son to the King of Naples

Gonzalo, an honest old Counsellor

Adrian and Francisco, Lords

Caliban, A savage and deformed Slave

Trinculo, A Jester

Stephano, a drunken Butler

Master of a Ship

Boatswain

Mariners

Miranda, daughter to Prospero

Ariel, an airy Spirit

Iris

Ceres

Juno, presented as Spirits

Nymphs

Reapers

Other Spirits attending on Prospero

THE STORY

A strange tempest wrecks a ship on an enchanted island ruled by the magician Prospero, the rightful Duke of Milan usurped and cast adrift fifteen years previously by his brother Antonio and the ambitious Alonso, King of Naples. Prospero lives with his daughter Miranda, their monstrous servant Caliban – son of a dead witch – and the sprite Ariel imprisoned by the witch and set free by Prospero.

Aboard the ship are all those who harmed Prospero – Alonso, and honest old Gonzalo who has remained loyal to him. With the help of Ariel, who must pay off his debt to Prospero, the magician separates crew and passengers, and then reveals himself to Ferdinand who proceeds to fall in love with Miranda. She returns his love, and the romance is approved by Prospero. Alonso's party search in vain for Ferdinand, and Antonio and Sebastian engage in still more plotting; Ariel hears them and reports back to his master. At this point, Caliban encounters the butler and the jester, Stephano and Trinculo, who proceed to get him drunk so that he becomes determined to rebel against his master Prospero.

Prospero draws together the various strands in the situation in a way in which wrongdoers are brought face to face with their actions and mercy prevails over vengeance. Alonso gives his blessing to the marriage of Ferdinand and Miranda, the traitors are forgiven, and Prospero prepares to return to Milan as its rightful Duke. At the play's end, Prospero releases Ariel from his service, returns the island to a chastened Caliban, breaks his magician's staff and buries his books. All will sail for home, guided by the gentle winds Ariel has conjured up, and with the audience's blessing as this is solicited by Prospero himself.

(Adapted from Fletcher and Jopling, 1989)

CHAPTER 1
What Islands Say

(a)   Landscapes

"Whether one is conscious of it or not," says Christy Newton "the ever-present and inundating usual signs and symbols of the social world perform a socializing function, reminding people who they are and where they are" (2009:1). Nowhere is this more the case than with islands. An island focuses, concentrates, reminds, inspires; it brings us up short against the matter in hand. It is not surprising therefore that Prospero works his magic on an island. As Robinson Crusoe demonstrated, an island is a human cosmos waiting to be created.

If you ask somebody to draw an island for you on a piece of paper they will almost certainly give it a set of geographical features – a river, a forest, perhaps a swamp or a lake, almost certainly a mountain peak. Islands demand these things, or at least the ones which we draw seem to do. Perhaps it is something about conjuring up that substantial expanse of sea on which islands rely in order to be themselves; geographical features must be included in order the show the nature of the contrast: this is land, real land, terra firma, a sure foothold – for what are boats but imitation islands. All this is expressed by making a mark on a piece of paper and then drawing attention to its particular significance, that it points towards a very important difference in the conditions which sustain life or even, for us, make life sustainable at all.

1

Islands draw attention to fundamental truths about being human. Our drawing may be crude and lacking realistic detail of any kind, but it is certainly intentional – in order to be authentically an island this shape must contain these objects, not for purposes of geographical accuracy, but because we simply feel they belong there, as part of the island. If you try leaving them out – if there is no river or forest or lake or canyon, worst of all, if people can't find the mountain, someone will immediately say where is it, why have you left it out? They may even try to draw it in for you, a shapely Mount Fuji between the forest and seashore.

Fujiyama of course is a special mountain, the object of religious veneration. Not everyone includes a shrine in their imaginary island. In a way they don't need to because islands have their own holiness simply by being the most potent symbol people use in order to express the human experience of standing apart, separating ourselves in the most effective way so that we no longer make any kind of contact with whomever or whatever we have journeyed away from; *more* effective than any kind of wall or barrier which while it separates also actually holds together. Oceans do not mediate; they are the nearest we can get, in tangible terms, to empty space. The island itself speaks of human experience in language too deep for words; and this is something else which lies in with its geographical furniture. It is symbolic by association, the mountain of mountain-ness, the forest of forest-ness, the lake of lake-ness, etc. in the same way and to the same degree as the island-ness which presents and focuses them.

This is a kind of implied sacredness, the kind which attaches to certain key aspects of human awareness, things which possess meaning-behind-meaning. "Because sacred aspects of life symbolise, contain or point to something that lies beyond themselves", says Kenneth Pargament, "they are more than simple objects (2007:14). We could put this another way by saying that they are factual and poetic at the same time; and anything which is capable of being both can be, and is, a vehicle for messages which are nonetheless powerful for being impossible to tie down. Anything we can isolate may be used as the sign for more than its single self; this is obvious of course, and human thought makes no sense, cannot be used to make sense apart from it. All the same, the fact remains that some things point beyond themselves more than others; and that these things stand out from the general order of things capable of signifying more than their immediate meaning. These are so powerfully symbolic that they seem to point beyond themselves even more than to themselves, except in a contributory way. We identify these as spiritual symbols, as symbols of spirituality, and associate them with actual religions because of the profundity of the presence that they possess for us – their effect upon us which seems to change the quality, subtly or dramatically, of the way we experience being alive. Such symbols direct us to a hidden reality, one which is not customarily present to awareness, whose reference is to itself, its own distinctive and profound identity which it is somehow able to share with us; which is the very stuff of religion.

It would, however, be a mistake to conclude from this capability of symbol that such things resonate only for people who recognise themselves as religious; whether or not they subscribe to a particular religion or find meaning in the idea of transcendence as such, except when brought face to face with this kind of irresistible 'otherness'. The religious identity of such symbols remains implicit, even though their sacredness presents itself as an experienced reality, as undisputable as their ordinariness, which it manages to subsume without in any way cancelling out. Indeed the dynamic of symbolism depends upon its preservation. Some of the natural expressions of this sacredness seem to owe their force to the fact that they blow our minds through sheer size or intensity of impact. Sacredness does not in itself depend on impressiveness of this kind, although sometimes the vehicles it inhabits are undeniably imposing – mountain, forests, rivers, canyons. As Pargament points out, "People are capable of instilling virtually any aspect of life with spiritual significance and meaning" (2007:41). Perhaps this is because sacredness happens between beings; it is not something attributed to an object, but something which reveals an event, an occasion, a presence to Otherness, of which we are reminded by a particular aspect of life, a specific object. As Paul Tillich wrote "The encounter with the holy, in its essence, is not an encounter beside other encounters, it is within the others" (1967: 128) – within them, responsible for what they are, what they lead us into being.

The religion of natural symbols must be implicit. An experience of signs not statements, in some ways as frustrating as it is inspiring. Implicit should not be taken to mean unstated, but stated in a different way, one which is if anything more powerful than other linguistic codes. In this sense 'implied' refers to the way we learn by our involvement within a situation, which is learning about the situation itself as distinct from drawing definite conclusions from it (which would qualify as 'explicit'). Thus 'implicit' can mean contextual, shedding any suggestion of concealment in favour of a sense of belonging within something. This kind of implicitness refers to 'understanding within a landscape'. Learning things which only this landscape can teach.

(b)   The Island and its Visitors

It is, however, one which is already known to us. Things of prime importance are presented as scenarios – people and objects within a time and place – not because such things need dramatising but because their significance renders them dramatic, so that to heighten their implicit drama in any way, standing back in order to do so in a way which makes us observers rather than participants, is to refuse to accept the personal significance they intrinsically hold for us. When we make our scenarios explicit, giving them the shape and intentionality we ourselves bring to them, it is this underlying spiritual force, implicit in our spontaneous apprehension of 'natural symbolism' which we manipulate by the paradox of aesthetic distance – the trick of standing back in order to feel more drawn in than ever.

The present book owes its genesis to both these kinds of implied symbolism: a play – Shakespeare's The Tempest – and the reality of islands and the natural symbolism which this provides – an archetypal source of meaning for the playwright, providing a background of transpersonal resonance and emotional power. As has often been said, the chief player in Shakespeare's drama is in fact the island itself, the undergirding significance of the milieu in which the action takes place. Life on the island brings about an intensity of experience which, to borrow Berger's and Luckman's phrase, "acts back upon nature" (1967:183). Our apprehension of our surroundings reflects the ideas and feelings we have about ourselves; we find ourselves attending to our experience of the natural world in a way and at a level which literally defies analysis. Indeed the very thought that such a thing might be happening makes us wary of the ridicule of sensible people, which is why we defend ourselves by protesting that what we are describing is not to be taken too seriously. After all everybody knows that features of a landscape are inanimate, and that poetic talk about communion with nature should not be taken literally.

Nevertheless, landscapes and settings do seem to 'talk' to us, and our natural response is to imagine ourselves talking back in some way. It has been suggested that the messages received are actually encoded by the recipients; certainly it makes an ordinary kind of sense to see ourselves generating a response in order to receive back things we want to hear

– comforting assurances of purpose and hope, which we may take as evidence that we are not alone in the universe. Admittedly these things stand out more clearly when the natural surroundings strike us with a sense of awe or transport us by their beauty. At the time however we tend not to be so convinced by this kind of argument, usually dismissed as the 'pathetic fallacy'. It seems, then, to be more likely that the message of the mountains and lakes is their own – one which concerns us but authentically not one generated by ourselves. Perhaps it is one which we have forgotten or managed to disregard, so that we have to have it brought home in this powerful way using a language implicit in reality itself. The more convincing attempt to make sense of this transcendent language speaks of a species-characteristic way of apprehending universal truth which naturally communicates in terms of the universe and what it contains: Jung's collective unconscious. Mountains, rivers, wells, forests, like earthquakes, tornados and tidal waves, are archetypal symbols of transpersonal meaning.

Whether this is true in any literal sense, the features of the island landscape remind the ship-wrecked mariners of the factual nature of their human embodied existence; and do so by bringing them into the presence of something able to direct their awareness towards 'the ground of their being'. This is a profound experience which can have a lasting effect on the way they regard life from then on, and it remains closely associated with the circumstances of that first encounter. This is not simply a figure of speech, a useful way of giving a hand-me-down significance to whatever it may be that we are talking about – the features of our imaginary landscape – which is less easily to hand for precisely such a purpose, and whose actual effect may be to make communication less immediate by distancing us from the matter in hand so that the stuff of real poetry becomes a mere 'figure of speech'.

The effect of actual encounters with nature is very different from this. Some experiences stay particularly vivid, giving rise to images which exist on another plane altogether, and which it is hard to be specific about because they possess the power to defy analysis; the urge to stand back and draw conclusions as to why one mountain may move me to tears while another simply impresses me with its sheer size. This, again is a well documented phenomenon. The idea of transcendental presences in nature, or nature's ability to point beyond itself to a more fundamental truthfulness, is familiar to students of religion, and of course worshippers themselves, but the actual presence of this mysticism, its experienced reality, can very easily be lost in the search for expression of the inexplicable. Adrian Cooper, commenting on the descriptions of those who have spent time wandering in mountain wildernesses, cites one mountaineer's conclusion:

> A lot of that mountain inspiration really transcends the limits of any religion, because what I'm learning is more fundamental, and more common to human wisdom than any specific doctrine. (1997:69)

On an island, of course, the mystery of mountains is never able simply to fade into the background. Indeed, from this point of view it could be said that an island is all foreground, such is the focusing effect of the surrounding ocean. One of Cooper's wanderers speaks of "A distinctive spiritual encounter with macrocosm and microcosm" which calls to mind the Japanese minimalist Haiku tradition. Certainly there is more to this island spiritually than a heightened sensory excitement. Heightening there certainly is, but there is also an overwhelming sense of wholeness, of the reincorporation of estranged life experiences, a feeling of somehow being given back to ourselves. It is of course possible to extrapolate such feelings into definite statements about the nature of truth; but this is not how they are actually communicated and received. This happens in ways which are easy to remember, difficult to tie down. This, of course, is the main reason for the influence such experiences have upon our lives, as they are able to accompany us on our journey. We do not move on from them, having registered their meaning and stored it away in our databank of useful things we have learned on our way through life; instead they move with us as perpetual reminders of times and places in which we found ourselves lifted beyond ourselves, all our questions answered; even the ones we never thought to ask in a way beyond imagination.

This then is the focused spirituality of mountains, which are of course, large natural features commanding our attention by their presence within any landscape. It is a spirituality which heightens our perception of other things in nature too, of course. It seems that once our attention has been seized by the presence of rocks and streams and lakes, plants, trees and wild creatures, a door may be opened in the universe and we see quite ordinary things in a new way: we see them as if we ourselves were new. Concentration on the other as other, as possessing its own life, transports us closer to it. We are aware of its unique reality as we bring our own to bear on it. Obviously size has little or nothing to do with this; it is the "heaven" we "see in a grain of sand".

Is this heaven something in ourselves or in the object of our attention. How much is that object actually a subject? The personal being which nature possesses, and which is experienced in a focused way in island landfalls is no cognitive communication. It is sensed by us as something happening between, but in no way is its message explicit. Its significance lies in the novel way it reaches us, through channels of human perception which are discounted and often ignored altogether. If, as some people believe, this sharing constitutes religion, then the language which it uses to make its presence felt is implicit not explicit. Those who draw inspiration from their natural surroundings in this way may be described as investing in the implicit. Whether or not their attitude actually becomes a religious one will depend on the degree to which it affects their lives; and this is where the island plays its major role simply by being itself – an island, a world set aside from normal view and thereby subject of a more intense scrutiny, a place shut away so that it can open itself up, revealing what is normally kept hidden.

This, at least is how Prospero's island appears to the King's son Ferdinand:

> Where should this music be? I' th'air or th'earth?
> Sitting on a bank
> Weeping, again the king my father's wrack
> This music creeps by me on the waters,
> Allaying both their, and my passion.

"Full fathom five thy father lies", sings Ariel, and Ferdinand listens in wonder at the strangeness of it all:

> This is no mortal business, nor no sound that the earth
> owes. (Act I sc.2)

What happens on this island involves a transformation in the lives of those involved in the story of Prospero and Miranda. It is a change of the order of that taking place when living flesh and bone become sea coral. Not that it is explicitly religious in the way it is presented; the narrative is implicitly religious to the degree that its telling is spiritually creative. Here religiousness subsists in the island's interaction with those who visit it. This island is open to the character of the people involved. Each will find it speaking to her or his state of soul. "O brave new world that hath such people in it," proclaims Miranda with the amazement of innocence

(Act V sc.1), while for old Gonzalo arriving on dry land brings relief and reassurance, the island presenting itself as fresh and alive. Not so however for Sebastian and Antonio, both of them cynically ambitious and in search of the main chance, who see the isle solely as an unfortunate hiatus in their journey to power:

Gonzalo: Here is everything advantageous to life
Antonio: True – save means to live
(Act II sc.1)

The question is whether an experience which focuses one's sense of being oneself in this vivid way may be described as implicitly religious? Or is it simply deeply spiritual? The psychoformative presence on the island is certainly a crucial factor; more important still is the drama which unfolds upon it. In fact it is impossible to separate these things in any meaningful way. The shipwrecked courtiers as well as the lovers themselves have, as far as the audience is concerned, become part of a single event; however we regarded them to begin with, by the end of the play they are now authentically 'creatures of the island' almost as much as Ariel and Caliban, the difference being that their creatureliness is recognizably their own, a new life emerging from the island experience, not simply a device of Prospero's. It is what they themselves bring to the island which gives the play its life – the way it reflects them to themselves.

Certainly this kind of renewed selfhood implies religious awareness on the part of those involved in the island experience, so that the metaphorical impact of the island, its poetic role in the play, appears as a background to actual change in the way the characters now experience themselves and one another. We sense them as being more real, more human, more alive, in fact. If the intensity of our engagement with things human is a hallmark of implicit religion, then powerful evidence of religious conversion is to be found on Prospero's island. The island itself has become a crucible of commitment, a place of focused self-discovery, and an integrating presence; in other words 'an intensive concern with extensive effects' (Bailey, 2001).

If Prospero's island is anything to go by – and we have been arguing that such is very much the case – islands may act as theatres for the unfolding of the drama of human awareness. Used metaphorically they are capable of helping change reality and to do this at a profoundly personal level. They are symbols of a transformation which may be seen as implicitly religious; and this is their importance for those involved in pastoral care.

(c)   Islands of Caring

Most people involved in pastoral care would agree that it is not meant to be a form of religious indoctrination. At the same time it is certainly concerned with human spirituality, which may or may not be associated with allegiance to any specific religion. Islands signify beyond-ness which, in the presence of human caring, spells hope for emotionally wounded people and nurturing for those bruised by life – those who need to come, or perhaps be brought in, from the storm. The notion of actually bringing people 'in' certainly has unfortunate overtones of missionary activity, which may not be the carers' intention but is easily assumed to be so by the person she or he is trying to help. 'Pastoral care' and 'pastoral theology' sound similar but are actually quite different. Describing the latter, Emmanuel Larbey reminds us that

> Pastoral theology has been an essential part of attempts by
> faith communities to embody, enflesh and refine the acts of
> love and care they engage in as an expression of their faith.
> (2006:3)

Frank Wright, on the other hand, sees pastoral care as less explicitly instrumental than this, which involves

> A transcendental reality... and a conviction that the path to
> wholeness is not purely of human endeavour and through
> the interaction of human beings. It is sufficient, however,
> that that dimension is silently present, without any self-
> conscious references. (1980:9)

By 'self-conscious' he is referring to the practice of religious people to make perfectly sure that the person whom they are trying to help knows that they are doing it for purposes which are explicitly religious, the suggestion being that if this were not the case, then they would probably not have become involved! What they do to help is an expression of their faith, one which is considered by them to be the most effective way of letting it be seen, and presumably emulated by anyone willing to take notice, but first and foremost the object of care themselves.

It has to be said that this approach is not always an effective way of spreading the gospel, particularly with regard to emotionally vulnerable people, who are more likely to be affected by the implied than the explicit, by things they themselves discern than those specifically displayed.

Vulnerable people are open to attempts to influence them certainly; but an essential aim of pastoral care is to allow those receiving it to find healing for themselves. This can only be done if the carers' main aim is acceptance, not conformity – any kind of conformity, even the explicitly religious belonging which they themselves so whole-heartedly recommend and sponsor. Theology, pastoral theology, educates carers; pastoral care itself simply provides a place set apart for healing.

An Island

Hence the purpose of this book, which takes some of the aspects of pastoral care and sees them in terms of the characteristics possessed by the islands. In the following chapters the image of the island stands as a metaphor for the human condition at its most vulnerable and also its most creative. The inspiration was Shakespeare's play The Tempest, but the aim is not literary criticism but dramatic exploration – exploration, a theme – a theme brought vividly to life by 'a master playwright' and its application to pastoral care. Prospero has a particular purpose for his island, involving a good deal of careful preparation. It is important to recognise that what he sets about creating is not the island itself – even his magic does not stretch as far as that – but a special use for it. In fact he works as metteur-en-scène of a drama of confrontation, recognition and repentance whose overall theme is renewal rather than revenge, for as he says

> The rarer action is
> In virtue than in vengeance: they being penitent
> The sole drift of my purpose doth extend
> Not a frown further. Go release them Ariel,
> My charms I'll break, their senses I'll restore,
> And they shall be themselves. (Act V sc.1)

"And they shall be themselves". Not everybody's island will possess the same shoreline as Prospero's; but one of the purposes of pastoral care will be to provide distressed or defeated souls with the island-space they need in order to act out their own uniquely personal scenario of human relationship.

To sum up this first chapter, therefore, what is mainly to be learned from islands in general, and Prospero's in particular. It is the vital importance of setting the scene for healing to take place just as on the island, the surroundings themselves both inspire and also reassure; so in the practice of pastoral care a particular quality of personal relationship is embodied in a special way of regarding another person, one best described as a sustaining presence, comforting yet challenging: a kind of therapeutic expectancy of changes yet unspecified. Only those who set out on this journey are in a position to know where it will lead or how long it may take them to arrive. Pastoral care of this kind is not time-limited, except in circumstances which force it to be so. It is a nurturing process rather than an explicitly educational one. The change involved is the kind which resists the overt pressure to conform. It lives in, and depends upon, the quality of personal relationships: of healing friendship encouraging self regard in the light of the respect and concern evident in someone else's attitude.

- I don't know exactly what I expected. I'm not a religious person at all you see, and religious people usually make me rather angry, assuming all sorts of things about me without really knowing me at all. This was different though. There was someone there to talk to when I wanted them, but not when I didn't. I didn't have to talk ... (Psychotherapy client – an ex nun)

- It's when you didn't know what you'd been searching for, and you find it ... (Answer to a questionnaire asking people to define spirituality)

- It's a kind of meeting – a person, a place, a work of art. You don't know what it is exactly until you meet it, and even then you can't be sure; but it's not like anything else. (The same questionnaire)

- I felt as though I'd come home at last – as though I could let myself come home. Up to then I just stayed closed up in myself, as if I didn't dare think or feel anything.

It may seem a long way from this kind of painful vulnerability to the imaginary world of *The Tempest*. What has pastoral care to do with play-going? There is a very definite reason for using theatre to typify our approach to care. In theatre, healing is approached obliquely, via the action of shared imaginative involvement and works implicitly within the world created by the play. As Prospero reminds us in his Epilogue, without empathy there can be no theatre:

> Gentle breath of yours my sails
> Must fill or else my project fails...

From this point of view theatre provides a striking model for pastoral care, as we the audience find ourselves invited in without knowing what to expect, to receive healing which gets under our guard.

CHAPTER 2
Telling The Tale

Miranda: You have often
Begun to tell me what I am but stopped
And left me with a bootless inquisition. (*The Tempest* Act I sc.2)

CV

(a)   My Own history

I suppose I'd better tell you straight away that I've spent
the last seven years in prison. I ought to come clean about
that first of all. Before I tell you anything else about myself.
There's quite a lot to tell, but prison has crowded most of it
out. For me, prison takes precedence …

I met Stanley on a surgical ward at the hospital where I was working
with the Chaplaincy staff. He wasn't in hospital for long, just a couple of
days, but it gave him an opportunity to talk to somebody who seemed
willing to listen. He spoke a lot about his time in prison, where he had been
sent for embezzlement – 'working a scam', he called it – behaviour which he
assured me was by no means characteristic of the way in which he usually
tried to run his life. All the same prison had been something of a turning
point for him because it was there that he thought seriously about who
he was and what he really wanted to do with his life – a life which up to
now had seen basically lacking in discernible purpose. Or so he told me. I

13

realize that my being a clergyman almost certainly affected the tone of our conversation, or even the choice of events which made up his narrative; but it was he who buttonholed me, and not the other way round, and it was I who provided him with his first real opportunity to talk about what he felt was beginning to happen to him – the new quality of self-awareness which had begun to surface during those years in prison. I sat by his bed, there in the ward, and composed myself to listen to whatever he might say to me. Tell me about yourself, I said.

"You mean the history of my life? You don't want to hear all that."

"Not if you don't want to tell me. It's up to you."

It seemed that he did want. It is usually easy enough to get people to talk about things which have happened to them earlier in their lives, so long as they feel safe enough to do so, that is of course. In order to do it, they naturally order events in some kind of chronological succession. The kind of significance an event has depends largely on its relationship to whatever went before and came after it – particularly the latter; as Kirkegaard says "life is lived in the future and understood in the past" Talking about oneself in this way certainly increases one's sense of personal reality – life as something which can be grasped in the operation of describing it. Look, we say, this is *me* – and it is ourselves we are telling as well as the other person. Our presence to them, revealed in the attention they pay us when we tell them about ourselves makes our story – and consequently our self-hood – real.

This is the true creativity of story – its ability to make sense of life. In some way at a particular level of awareness, Stan discerned a relationship between those live periods in his life, the life lived through in prison, and the much shorter period he was now forced to spend on a hospital ward. He couldn't really explain this, but simply pulling the two events together made sense to him, a kind of narrative explanation which has no need for further investigation – and in fact trying to be verbally explicit about it seemed to obscure the message it transmitted so powerfully and clearly. Prison had been, or could now be seen to have been, a time for rediscovering things about himself which he had forgotten – "rediscovering myself" he said, and prison was a way of making the new/old Stan real. What had been gestating in prison now came to birth in hospital, as the pain and discomfort of a physical illness underlined the importance of a psychological change. As the pain receded, Stan said, he had recovered in more ways than one. This was not simply a chastened resolve to be a better person in the future, to "turn over a new leaf" (this took some explaining to a clergyman, you understand); it was more a case of having gained more trustworthy evidence about being a person at all.

Prison and hospital, put together, threw light on a lot of other things, too: the 'light of events which happen in sequence to illuminate' simply by the order in which they occur, so that it isn't a case of inventing a narrative but of being presented with one. This, at least is how it feels. Personal histories of this kind are not consciously conceived as explanations. If they were, they would not stand out in the way that they do, as solutions to unstated problems possessing a revelatory power which is global rather than simply intellectual. Certainly they change the way we think; but they do it by transforming the way we are with regard to ourselves. They work at the level of our sense of being by forming in us the awareness of having something intrinsically worth the effort to trying to explain.

The explanation we fall back on is in the form of a story. Stan spoke and I listened. When he had come to the end of the story he had to tell, that of how he had come to be in this particular ward of this particular hospital, and why he felt it to be so important with regard to him as a person, he thanked me for listening. It had been a gripping story and I had other wards to visit; I stood for a few moments in the busy hospital corridor before going on.

One of the things which my encounter with Stanley on the hospital ward brought home to me was the special significance of bodily awareness in the formation of personal stories. Narrative of a personal kind has the effect of embodying a sense of being which otherwise may remain vague and undeterminable; body and story suggest each other in a memorable way. In Gabriel Marcel's words I am unable to gain a real sense of bodily presence except in terms of the story of things which have happened to me because

> there is no relationship between story, myself as subject
> and my body that could be defined in an unequivocal
> and generally valid manner. I have to establish my own
> relationships with my body; I have to originate or even
> invent them. (1967:67)

(b) Flesh and Bone

Nowhere is the connection between story telling and embodiment brought so vividly to life as it is in drama. This is a subject which has been, and continues to be, explored at depth ever since the work carried out by David Grossvogel (1962) and Brian Wilshire (1982) and lately from a more explicably therapeutic angle by Phil Jones in Drama as Therapy: Theory, Practice and Research (2nd ed., 2007, vide also Mary Duggan and Roger Grainger, 1997). The argument about theatre as the embodiment of ideas about the experience of being human is presented most forcibly and unforgettably by plays themselves rather than books about them, of course. One notable example of this is Pirandello's Six Characters in Search of an Author, where the bodily presence of the stage personages aggressively asserts their human reality in the face of other people's assumption as to what they should be considered to be. The Tempest is an earlier example, and in some ways an even more powerful one, as its principal character demonstrates his identity not only as a creature but also as creator, the spinner of stories not merely a personage in someone else's. Prospero is not somebody who Shakespeare presents to the audience, to us, that is. He himself presents the unfolding drama of the storm and the world it brings into being as the stage he will use in order to present us with the story, inviting us to take part in it alongside the characters he has provided in order to be our temporary companions; but at the end he comes forward to greet us as himself – not a magician but a creature of flesh and blood; an actor, and, like ourselves, a teller of stories.

Scene One proclaims the play's action – a story set on an island; things separated from ordinary life, known as an ongoing process through time, by a radical interruption of human circumstances – a storm resulting in a shipwreck. The end of predictable, understandable, plannable, events; the shipwreck of the ordinary. Seen as an event – and it must be in order for it to be lived through at all, a totally unprepared-for happening. No way of reacting but by acceptance; but from now on nothing may be approached and managed in the old way, because of this caesura in the perceived universe experienced by those involved as the immediate circumstances involved in being alive, being human. Within the story-telling dimension of experience, the explanations we arrive at when thought is restored and things have settled down again our experience of being human is closely connected with, or even dependent upon the saga of collapse and reordering, defeat and re-assertion which we recognise to some or other extent in every story ever told.

Now we can stand back from events, in a systematic way, so that we are able to tell the tale both to ourselves and other people, reinforcing our new way of presenting ourselves. This has been painfully put together but now possesses the comforting sense of order and purpose which can only be present when the work of reconstruction has achieved some measure of success.

Literary and dramatic fiction is usually described as a way of making sense of human experience by demonstrating a tendency which to some degree we all possess, that of surprising ourselves by discovering meaning where we have no idea that it can possibly exist. This, however, is not an invention of those whose particular job in life is to relieve our sense of confusion or discouragement by their own special ability to craft alternative endings to our personal dilemmas and then somehow find ways of selling them to us. We are our own authors and playwrights. Our truth and our fiction march hand in hand, our ability to attain the first dependent on our native skill in deploying the resources provided by the second. What we do in what we are accustomed to call 'real life' is precisely what is done for us in works of fiction. The fiction does not automatically relate to us; Prospero's island does not present itself in terms of a literal reproduction of our own experience. On the contrary we ourselves have to do this. When we read the play, or better still see and hear it acted for us, we make it part of our story to the extent that we recognise in it an expression of our own story-ness, the serious process of fictionalisation to which we owe a sense of selfhood.

(c) Setting

For human beings, story-ness lies everywhere, each story clustered round some dramatic interruption of life-as-we-know it, each moving at its own speed, so that stories overlap to the extent of swallowing each other up. The shipwreck which clears a narrative space for the tale of Miranda and Ferdinand provides a climax for the interrupted saga of Prospero and Antonio his ambitious brother. For sense to prevail story making is essential, and the collapse of personal meaning – the meaning according to which I know myself to be a person – can only be healed by my having something hopeful to say to myself about myself; a story which is able to present catastrophe as an essential requisite for self-being.

One way or another, stories must be told, and the best way of doing this is to tell them to others. My life, says Gabriel Marcel

> presents itself to reflection as something whose essential
> nature is that it can be related as a story ... and this is so
> very true that one may be permitted to wonder whether

the words 'my life' retain any precise meaning at all as we abstract from the meaning we attach to them any reference whatsoever to the act of narration. (1984:154)

Certainly this is the closest and most intimate relationship between narrative and lived experience. In the second scene of *The Tempest*, Prospero tells his daughter the story of their arrival on the island and the circumstances which gave rise to it. It does not take long to do this, a hundred and thirty lines in fact, but we are present while it is being done. We see and hear Prospero as he tells his daughter his story; tells her about himself, who he is and where he comes from, at the same time and by the same means informing her about *herself* too. This important section of the play's structure sets the scene for the ensuing drama as it demonstrates and embodies our characteristic way of sharing information about actual human life – not as data but narrative, things remembered and re-told.

Prospero: What seest thou else
In the dark backward and abyss of time?
If thou remember'st aught ere thou cam'st here
How thou cam'st here, thou may'st.

Miranda:But that I do not.

Prospero:Twelve years since, Miranda, twelve years since,
Thy father was the Duke of Milan, and
A prince of power...

Because of a cultural association of human truth with things which may be reliably demonstrated, we refuse to give narrative the regard it deserves as the very basis of our understanding of ourselves and other people. We prefer information obtained in other ways, seeing it as less biased and consequently more trustworthy. However it is the bias which holds our narratives together, preventing them from becoming strings of meaningless events, the raw material for a meaning which we have successfully sanitised away by our determination to remain impersonal, un-involved. Obviously drama sets itself firmly against this kind of impartiality, preferring to let us choose our own emotional responses to the cast of characters and range of stories presented to us. The sheer availability of story makes it the preferred medium of every kind of self-disclosure, as an endless series of narratives which are both true and provisional – stories about ourselves which may be either adopted or abandoned, but which, because they are stories rather than blueprints or specifications, retain their usefulness along with their identity not simply as a story, the image of a completer action, but as potentially our story. An unreliable blueprint is of no use to anyone: it is fixed, authoritative and wrong. Stories that are really personal are renewable, too.

In a sense, story is a way of interrupting time; stopping it in fact, by allowing experiences and the ideas associated with them to free themselves from the flux of events to be made sense of and lived with which has the inevitable effect of destroying their uniqueness – their graspability – by underlining their provisional, unfinished nature. Art, and particularly narrative art, makes statements which 'stand outside time' and can consequently be used to interpret its meaning without being compromised by its refusal to stay still. It permits something to happen as itself; something to be grasped by the mind and used to affect life instead of always being affected by it.

(d)   Transformation Scene

Story demonstrates in the clearest way the ability of the artistic imagination to encourage change in the way we look at life. It is essentially purposeful, being primarily concerned with endings, interruptions of the ongoing course of events in order to show how things turned out – and consequently with the possibility of new beginnings. Having a middle and an end actually and an end actually gives it a flexibility – not by portraying the variability of human experience, but by assisting closure and consequently providing space for new things to happen. Though the actual incidents recorded in the story itself may be 'drawn from life', the action of story-telling cuts directly across life.

In The Tempest, Shakespeare uses a story about an island in order to demonstrate the islanding effect of story itself, as inventive and surprising as imagination itself yet capable of communicating an assurance of meaning which continues to resist the shapelessness of its context, the ocean of life in the real world.

Not only Shakespeare of course. Story telling is a resource we all use when we wish to explore the meaning of our existence, or to communicate to others our own faith in the presence of such a meaning in the knowledge that this faith can change lives. Psychotherapists have grown increasingly aware of the possibilities of relieving psychological distress – healing damaged lives – by the creative use of story. David Willows describes stories as "agents of transformation". He quotes one told by Martin Buber – again a story about a story.

> An old rabbi sat on a chair among his friends in the shadow of the great temple. Wearied by his age and infirmity, the fraternity were well used to passing their time in discussion and debate. On this particular day, however, the rabbi chose not to entertain those around him with fine rhetoric and sophisticated logic. Instead, he began to tell them a story about his own teacher who used to perform all sorts of strange antics during the course of saying his prayers. This used to go on for considerable periods of time as the rabbi became increasingly taken up by his story, until, all of a sudden the rabbi altogether forgot his infirmity, stood up and began to jump and dance, just as his master had done. From that moment on, or so the story goes, the rabbi was healed. The story had transformed him. (2000:181)

What, then, is it about story which can have this powerfully transformative effect. Buber describes the transformation of the storyteller himself by the action of recall involved in the narration. He is very clear in his account that it is story rather than "discussion and debate", fine rhetoric and sophisticated logic, which has this amazing effect. The rabbi's listeners are confronted by an unforgettable demonstration of the power of story telling, in which the action of telling a story from our own past-experience reacts in a revolutionary way on our life in the present. As Buber's account shows very clearly, the degree of our involvement in our story telling is an important factor. In some way and at some level, the story we tell must possess real significance for us. Stories reveal and re-activate personal involvement. They are about what happens between and among people framed in a way which makes the significance of our interaction more readily available than it might otherwise be. The effect of storytelling is to provide a necessary medium for information of a potentially unwelcome kind – things which we would find psychologically threatening about ourselves and our relationships if they were to be communicated in a more directly personal way. The action of standing back from a situation and regarding it as a story about ourselves rather than a part of our immediate experience – what we are accustomed to call 'the here and now' – changes our perception of the material we are dealing with. The operative word is 'about'. In practical terms talking about me is less immediate than talking as me would be; so much so that in some situations I may be unwilling to disclose, even to myself, what it is that I really feel and think. Story telling has a fictionalising effect even when the story I am telling is about me; I have to withdraw from my immediate reality even in order to tell it, so that there is always something which links it to the stories we tell about other people. Drama and self-drama are both drama; consequently each of them may be used to authenticate the other, and both provide a way of defusing whatever is too painful to encounter, understanding of the truth about ourselves.

As Aristotle suggested, theatre encourages a healing access of emotional understanding which he identified as catharsis, or emotional purging. It does this because of the balance it allows between detachment and contact, the world of fiction and that of current actuality, a trade off which allows involvement to take place, as we recognise our own pain in that of the play's character, whose distance from ourselves is made obvious by the fictional nature of the action. Plays provide us with a place where it is safe to feel; and so obviously do the stories.

The first characteristic of story on which all the others depend is distance. We are encouraged by the story format to take account of other people and ourselves; we share a story with one another. In doing so we are able either explicably or implicitly, to share ourselves, in fact. This is why stories are memorable, possessing the authority of vivid personal experience – the experience of sharing the story as well as the things the story itself describes. Because of this they are able to become part of the way we perceive the world and ourselves in it.

Another fundamental characteristic of story is, of course, its openness to all kinds of modifications, some minor, provided in order to produce more 'fit' (increased relevance for and existing state of affairs) and some quite radical or even revolutionary, having the effect of totally altering the entire point of the story. Stories are flexible because of their nature as fiction; they can be used in the most intimate and precise ways to illuminate personal truth. Stories form alliances with one another so that the imaginative potential of story seems practically endless as particular themes may carry with them a weight of narrative force and allusive significance concentrated upon a central transcendence of actual inter or intra personal experience.

This kind of symbolism is not something which may easily be tied down; indeed that is the reason why it exists in the first place. Because of this it can have a distorting or a misleading effect. Stories can lie as well as tell the truth, using their independence of the actual to deny life as well as to promote it. Psychotherapists are painfully aware of this fact as clients cling tenaciously to a single punitive story about themselves and the message of hopelessness or disillusion which they receive from it. It is not easy to let go of a painful personal story, because although such stories are self-invented, they possess a factitious consistency of personal history; which of course is precisely what they were meant to do in the first place.

(e)   Making Sense of Life

Personal stories – the tales we tell ourselves about ourselves, and ram home by repeating to others – are essential ways of giving shape to otherwise inchoate experience. To this extent we are the stories we tell about ourselves and also, by implication, the ones we choose to tell and also to listen to about others. Story is thus both self-recognition and self-revelation. In the treatment of psychological distress associated with the traumatic disruption of personal universes; telling and listening to stories provides a way of approaching material which is too painful to be contacted head on. This is an area which has been explored by dramatherapists working to find ways of harnessing the 'as if' principle underlying every kind of theatrical presentation – the oblique involvement with others' stories which is able to release the emotional pressure exerted by the doubts and anxieties we have about ourselves – as a powerful kind of psychotherapy in its own right (Jennings, Cattenach, Mitchell, Chesner and Meldrum, 1994: Andersen-Warren and Grainger, 2000; Jones, 2007). The following scenario is an example.

> Rowena had spent many years as the companion of her widowed mother. When I met her she was forty-five, and in love for the first time in her life. Was it possible, she asked me, to change her own view of herself as a confirmed spinster, by marrying at this stage of her life? Marry she did, inviting her mother along to the wedding. Unfortunately her mother declined the invitation, dying shortly after, still refusing to speak to her daughter. Rowena came back in deep distress because of the unfinished business which now haunted her. Hers, she said, was a story which led nowhere at all, a drama without a climax. The central face-to-face encounter which would have been its turning point was missing. We began the task of creating a new story for Rowena. What was apparent to both of us was that no real

change could be achieved in the way Rowena thought and felt about herself unless we constructed our scenario around the factual nature of her mother's death. Somehow this must be built into our new scenario as its central idea, the thing her new story would be about. There turned out to be a good deal of material about her mother which Rowena wanted included which would throw light on her mother's attitude. At one point Rowena took on her mother's role "because it will help me understand her better when she dies". Gradually she put the two stories together, her own and her mother's – perceiving a new balance in the relationship between them, by putting her mother back in the space from which she felt she must be excluded. (Adapted from Grainger, 2006)

This sense of an excluded middle, a part of the argument which is missing which would somehow make sense of the whole. As Stephen Crites puts it "To become a self is to appropriate a past" (1986:164). The problem lies in choosing a past which is itself appropriate. Renewing Rowena's personal story involved a process of deconstructing a narrative in order to expose its apparent inevitability, which it owes to the way it hangs together, as in fact specious. We give our stories the probity bestowed by the process of story making, thereby selecting one possibility from all the materials we may have at hand for story construction; and then we suffer the consequences, as Rowena did, when she found herself sentenced to a role as someone who in a crucial personal relationship has somehow, as she put it, "missed the boat".

There are other ways of failing to achieve a satisfactory personal story, however, apart from this. A story is after all a story, and having a personal narrative bestows a sense of identity, described by Crites as "the depth dimension of the self" (1986: 171). Certainly, if I know who I am I can entertain the possibility of choosing to continue my progress through life in a different direction. This however is an option which only exists for those with a reasonably robust sense of identity, and who can say "I am the one who …" in a way which convinces themselves, if not other people.

Stephen Crites describes this inability to make sense of oneself as "the first [i.e. the most basic] type of unhappiness … the failure to appropriate my personal past by making a connected coherent story of it." A major player in the drama of self-construction is the human body itself, experienced as "a repository of memories, triumphs and reversals". Pius Ojara goes on to point to the close relationship between

'I am my body' and 'I am my past'. ... because bodiliness
historically is intrinsic to human personhood, individuality
and sociality' (2006: 237)

In there is a sense, it is our body which at the deepest, most personal
level 'holds us together'. Dramatherapists explore the relationship between
embodied experience and our sense of possessing our own identifiable
story.

Certain kinds of embodied experience have an effect on the way in which
we think and consequently feel about ourselves and our relationship to the
world we live in. Confused thinking and troubled or directionless behaviour
are symptomatic of each other. The relevance of this fact to drama seems clear
enough. Indeed a definition of drama might be 'the meaningful arrangement
of minds and bodies' – that is, a paradigm of purposeful human interaction.
For a dramatherapist's clients, the dramatic medium allows a measure of
first hand experience of sharing a closeness of personal contact which they
may previously have kept, both literally and metaphorically, at arms' length.
Dramatherapy involves the exploration of the dramatic medium at first hand
both as actors and audience, concentrating on the exchange of roles and the
interplay of personal perspectives embodied in story creation (Landy 1994;
Grainger 2006; Jones 2007; Langley 2006). Research carried out with people
whose thinking tended to be disordered in the sense that they had particular
difficulty in 'stringing ideas together', which made it hard for them to predict
their own and other people's behaviour in any given circumstances, showed
that experience of dramatherapy had the effect of making them more adept
at making associations and drawing conclusions:

> The structures of drama made use of the identical
> epistemological categories which govern our ordinary
> personal relationships, presenting them in the clearest
> possible way, while the overall dramatic convention provided
> the ontologically safe environment necessary for vulnerable
> people to take part. (Grainger 1992:178)

Drama promotes cognitive – and consequently emotional – clarity
because plays are patterned experiences, integral events, which are able to
draw us into the patterns they embody.

Plays are worked out in front of us and involve us in the working
out process. They promote the human experience of involvement in
patterned human relationship; that is, on things which 'work out' and 'hold
together'.

With this in mind, Prospero's island stands out vividly as the creation of a new, transformative story. It is transformative because it is itself about renewal. Presented within the here and now, it speaks to us about the future; its conflict and confusion are islanded in a vision of containment. Its message of new beginnings is encapsulated within its own action in the formal perfection of the masque Prospero creates to celebrate the burgeoning love between Miranda and Ferdinand; which acts as a pre-figuring of the play's final resolution when there is no longer any need for reality to be suspended, even temporarily, as the world has been restored to a condition of wholeness. Prospero "abjures his rough magic" because the need for invention is over. All the same, however, for those who have found themselves visiting his island his gift for story telling has proved to be satisfactory.

The island has been both a story in itself and the setting for a story, played out in all the things which have happened there. From a pastoral point of view, its own identity as the symbol of the story and storytelling is the most important thing about it. Metaphorically speaking stories are islands: their special this special kind of reality emerging out of the ocean of the factual, the common material of our literal existence. They are still part of our experience of life, just as the island is part of the concrete universe which contains the ocean surrounding it. Their fictional, provisional reality is transformed by absorption into the reality of our personal experience, its identity as story remaining as the outward sign of a deeper submerged truth – one which we only discover when, for one reason or another, as exploration landfall or shipwreck we find ourselves setting foot in territory which is distanced yet immediate, alien yet recognisable all the same. For many this kind of exploration of personal story is identical with their main purpose in life. At its most basic it is nothing other than the search for meaning which gives life its deepest purpose and justification. In Viktor Frankl's words, "Meaning must not coincide with being; meaning must be ahead of being. Meaning sets the pace for being" (1973: 22). As an island of sense in a sea of confusion, story allows a space for this to happen.

Prospero: Be collected.
No more amazement. (Act I sc.2)

Prospero's island is emblematic of the union of opposites which is characteristic of story itself. Like the island, story is focused freedom, concentrated possibility, the narrow way opening up between worlds. Its symbolism directs us to the practiced and imaginative use of story in pastoral care. Stories claiming to express truth which is universal or transcendent may be used to unlock those which are personal and consequently seen as private. They will only do so, however, if they are opened up for exploration and the possibility of discovery. An explicitly religious story, one about the incursion of transcendence into human experience may seize our attention, but will only have its intended effect on us if we are somehow encouraged to find a way of making it our story too. Pastoral care of a directly religious kind should be fully aware of this when it sets about telling its own story. Prospero's island points us towards an adventurous way of rediscovering familiar stories in which we allow ourselves to become part of the narrative itself, re-enacting our own stories in the light of our involvement in the mega-narrative, so that instead of standing over against the text we allow ourselves, for a short time at least, to live and work inside it, dramatising it in terms of our own experience.

> This is not the way we have usually been led to regard
> religious texts, which have been presented to us as sources
> of instruction rather than invitations to share in an
> experience which will lead us beyond ourselves. This has
> not prevented these stories from being a rich source of
> inspiration; of a deeply transforming by personal kind;
> but it has not helped either. Working together in groups
> provides an alternative to being told in advance what a
> text means, and how it is relevant to the listener. In group
> work what is valuable is not so much the conclusion arrived
> at – at their concordance with 'official' interpretations – as
> experience of simply sharing the journey. Telling people
> what they must look for in a text turns out to be a less than
> efficient way of sharing a personal experience of discovering
> where, for them, the focus of the story lies; which is
> the only way of really hearing about what it has to say.

(Grainger, 2000:2)

CHAPTER 3
Retreating To Advance

a. It's me I'm talking about
 Only I know who I am
 Only I know what I feel
 You say you know how I feel, and perhaps you do feel
 Something like it
 I wouldn't know, would I?
 Only you know who you are
 What you really are ...

It takes a 'user of psychiatric services' to remind us of something which professionals sometimes tend to forget. And yet it is obviously true. If perception is based on experience, and everybody's experiences have been different from everybody else's, then our judgements will all be different too – and if we judge differently we also experience differently. Somewhere in this circular process we notice things in other people's experiences which we recognise in our own, and we conclude from this that we know what they're feeling. Logic should then tell us that this cannot actually be true, that their experiencing history must be different from ours and their present feeling also different. Recognition is more convincing than logic however. We recognise enough to allow ourselves to contribute our feelings to theirs.

Thank God we do, of course. If we were always conscious that their worth was uniquely theirs – in the analytical way described above – we would forfeit the best part about being human; we would not in fact be human at all. We see, we recognise, we involve ourselves, and even if our recognition turns out in some particulars to be 'off the mark', our involvement is still effective, still brings us into relation. What we do recognise accurately is the presence of pain, calling forth sympathy; and, when we get to know someone better, or allow ourselves to be drawn closer to them, its specific quality – and this is what we know as empathy. Empathy is the recognition of how the heart is hurting. As such it cannot be described, only felt. However its cognitive unintelligibility is as vital as its emotional immediacy.

Genuine empathy brings home the fact that the other person is genuinely an other. The experience of empathy is a sudden bridging of a gap between I and Thou, a shaft of wordless light, a kind of emotional lean into someone else's story as distinct from an action of intellectual categorisation: "I can see you're hurting. Can I help?" rather than "I know how it feels" which always seems to imply "I've seen cases like yours before".

The voyage of discovery in which people set out from different personal universes to encounter each other in a new, shared experience is the most healing element in pastoral care, or in any other form of counselling or psychotherapy. If we think we know too much about the other person, who they are and where they've been, we may never set out on the healing journey at all: certainly never achieve the empathic break-through which comes from telling someone else to be themselves.

Only I know who I am.

On this occasion as on many others this was construed as a plea for understanding, hard enough to satisfy because the person asking never actually seemed understandable; never seemed willing to allow herself to be understood. Those trying to help her were quite sure that this was something she was actually doing on purpose, so that she could blame them for not understanding her. In other words, not being understood fulfilled some hidden purpose, the fulfilment of which provided her with some kind of personal satisfaction. She kept saying she was misunderstood because she enjoyed the attention it won her, as more and more people tried – and failed – to discover what she meant.

They were quite wrong. What she wanted was to be left alone to be herself in peace, so that she could somehow find out for herself what it was that was happening to her. To be allowed to make her own sense of what was happening to her without the help of other people to whom it wasn't happening and who couldn't know. To be un-understood in fact, by anyone other than herself. To force what was happening to make some kind of sense for her. I know this is so because she told me. In fact this was far harder than she thought it would be – her own thoughts weren't all that much more helpful for easing the pain than other people's were; she found that she did in fact need other people's help. All the same it was she who would ask, in her own way, when she was ready.

Andrew's story illustrates this very well. Andrew was not a 'user'. In fact he was a 'carer' as well as being a Charge Nurse in a local hospital. He had been married earlier on in his life, but things had not worked out, and in his mid forties he found himself doing two jobs – his work in the hospital and "keeping an eye on" – Andrews own phrase – his ageing mother.

When my mother died it was a very great blow to me. She was in her late eighties, and people said "Well she had a good innings, didn't she?" They didn't say this to me but I knew it was what they were all thinking, and it was what the Vicar said, more or less, at the funeral. Mother was what they call 'strong minded'. I didn't actually live with her, thank God, but I saw a good deal of her, particularly after my father died twenty years ago, and I used to pop round to see her every day during the last few years. She didn't like people doing things for her, but of course I did do more and more as time went on. "I keep an eye on you, you know," she used to say, and she did too. Sometimes it seemed I didn't have any private life at all.

So in a way it was a relief when I saw the coffin depart and the doors close. I didn't know where to put myself. There's a bereavement counsellor attached to the hospital and I thought of going to get some help. People said to me Andrew, you need help; see if you can get some counselling – and in fact I did go and see this nice friendly lady, who said I should try and talk about my mother. And I did try, and it did help a bit, I suppose, but there was so little to say really, nothing I could say to the counsellor except my mother's dead. She isn't there any more. Anything else was too trivial to mention. The counsellor couldn't do anything except sit and watch me struggling to digest the truth. So finally I said, it's no good, I can't say anything relevant at all. I can't talk about my mother when she's not there …

> I told the counsellor that I'd go away and work on it by
> myself. That's what I said, that I would work on it in my
> own time. And this is what I've tried to do. After a bit I
> found I could actually talk about my mother when people
> asked me 'how I was getting along in my bereavement', but

I couldn't actually think about her at all at first; there were
so many things said and regretted on both sides, so much
unfinished business … I remembered what I promised the
counsellor that I would really try and work on the problem,
so that I could at least remember her a bit. Remember her
as she really was, and I made myself remember bit by bit,
starting with the good bits, the happy bits, and going on
to the unhappy times when she refused to see my point of
view, and I wouldn't, or couldn't see hers.

When she did begin to come back it was in her own way,
at her own speed. It wasn't reading books and going on
bereavement courses, or all the advice people gave me – out
of the kindness of their hearts, I'm sure – it was working
through it all, keeping a tryst with it. I can't say it's all
cleared up, like some sort of infection; it was and is much
more personal than that. The loneliness and the sadness
still tends to hang around from time to time. But it should,
shouldn't it? If it's really part of my life, like she was.

The drawbacks of the sympathetic approach come across clearly in
Andrew's story. "I know how it feels. I've been there myself." – except that
you haven't, and you don't. The circumstances may appear to you to be
almost exactly congruous, certainly; but they were your circumstances, and
these were Andrew's. If you emphasize the sharedness you inevitably come
across as trying to underplay the uniqueness. This was Andrew's mother
and Andrew's grief; and like everyone else who suffers a deeply personal
loss, only Andrew could work through it. First of all however, it had to
be identified as his own, which meant fighting off others' attempts to get
in on the act. This may seem unduly harsh, but it is true nevertheless. Of
course we may express sympathy – but we should be careful how to do it.
It takes time to work through these things and work is something we do
ourselves.

Prospero

No one can construct another person's shattered world. We do not
keep the different aspects of our awareness in separate compartments. So

far as our conscious life is concerned the mind's organization resembles a web more closely than it does a bookcase. To use Construct Theory language, 'people-constructs' play more important roles in the preservation of our psychological integrity than do 'thing-constructs' (Kelly 1991); our superordinate constructs, the ways of thinking which organise our personal weltanschauungen are concerned with personal relationships, and to lose one of these disturbs our entire view of life until other connections can be made which will be able more or less to perform the same function within our psychic economy. Freud refers to "The work of mourning in which the ego is absorbed" (1917) as it reasserts its function of making tolerable sense of life particularly with regard to our relationships with others apart from ourselves; in this case others on whom our happiness depends. The work of reconstruction – of reconstruing the world of which we are part – is the hardest psychological work we ever have to do; and the most valuable gift we can receive from those around us is the space in which to do it.

At the end of The Tempest, when his island's task is complete and its purpose achieved, Prospero permits himself one final gesture. In a way it is for him the most difficult one of all, even harder than that of quelling his magical powers, which realised it in the first place.

Now my charms are all o'erthrown
And what strength I have's mine own
Which is most faint.

The renunciation of his magical power is, of course, all the more painful because it is entirely unforced, an action of voluntary self-denial. One can only conclude that he does it because his hidden magic is no longer necessary to him, that it somehow gets in the way of his real identity. At the end of the play Prospero emerges as his true self. This is a definite, fully personal, action, signifying a new stage in the story of his life. The purpose of the island and the events which have taken place on it becomes exceedingly clear at this point. Prospero tells the audience what he is going to do – "I'll burn my book – and then, after the final scene reports that, this is what he has done – "Now my charms are all o'erthrown". The Island and the effect it has had on those who have been the characters in its story or spectator-participants in its drama is now a *fait accompli*. No one is more aware of this than Prospero, the story's author and originator, who is now left high and dry with no-one to be but himself. His real identity as Duke of Milan awaits him; but for a brief moment he slips forward to greet the audience as particularly undefended, abandoning any kind of character armour, either that he has himself assumed as magician, the possessor of special powers denied to other men or that bestowed upon him by the accident of birth, his dukedom.

Prospero's identity depends not on his private skills and the disguise he is able to assume, but upon the justified expectations of other people that he is who he says he is. This involves a change in the person whom he sees himself being. It can only come about through his willingness to divest himself of the persona he has assumed as magician and wonder worker and stand revealed before us as someone without any character armour at all, admitting the fact he cannot be himself without our permission. This median condition of being 'neither one thing nor the other' is the requirement of all genuine existential change. The drama makes it clear by demonstration rather than argument, as it leaves Prospero's future entirely in the hands of his audience. Only they can enable him to complete his true task, which is that of discovering himself – locating the real Prospero:

> I must be here confin'd by you,
> Or sent to Naples. Let me not,
> Since I have my dukedom got
> And pardon'd the deceived, dwell
> In this bare island by your spell. (Epilogue)

The audience give Prospero back to himself by their applause. This, for him is the sign of their approval and commendation.

What is being asked for, and bestowed, here is permission to start again and any kind of instruction as to how to do so. It has been Prospero's story. Certainly we have found ourselves involved, but as privileged participants not actors. Prospero speaks as the protagonist in his own drama. Seen like this, in terms of theatre, the division between actors and audience is quite clear; it has been exaggerated so that the idea of the subject – the story of Prospero and Miranda – may stand out most clearly and with the greatest definition and strike home to us most forcibly, disarming our defences by respecting our privacy. We go away and reflect, perhaps even for the rest of our lives. Prospero, in the fictional reality Shakespeare has created, begins his labour of reconstruction.

If we ask how this applies to our own 'user of psychiatric services' and the way we, as pastoral carers, find ourselves regarding him, we may have to use our imagination a little to see anything more than a fanciful connection, more to do with literary criticism than it is with what we are used to calling 'real life'. In fact this is not really so at all. Our imaginations are crucially important every time we are asked to listen to some else's story or, of course, when we find ourselves invited to share our own story with them. Prospero's experience has a great deal to teach us here, if only because he places himself in the hands of his hearers and asks their help in assuring himself of his own continuing reality – his reality for himself, that is.

As we saw, this endorsement of selfhood takes place in an exchange of stories rather than the simple straightforward act of narration. We cannot tell our story unless we are aware of being really received. At the deepest most reflective level we must have this assurance; otherwise the urge to open ourselves up to be healed will continue to be frustrated. What we call empathy turns out from this angle to be an implied offer to swap stories. We may be very much aware of a whole range of inhibiting factors, the most obvious being the danger of our responsiveness actually having a negative effect by making it impossible for the other person to make themselves heard; as when we take centre stage and turn the spotlight on ourselves: "What you're saying reminds me about when I etc." This is something which theatre brings home very strongly; we are not encouraged to move into the acting area ourselves however much we may feel drawn into the action and feel we have to contribute to it, but our involvement is nevertheless necessary to the actors and gives the world being created the blessing of its own truth. Whether we are telling the story itself or listening to it we give ourselves to the action and forget our own agenda until the roles are reversed.

But what has the theatre to do with the situations we encounter in the ordinary business of caring for one another? Usually we tell ourselves that the pain of those we care for pastorally is real, whereas that of theatrical characters is an illusion, and in the long run should not be taken seriously. All the same, we do take it seriously and the resulting pain we ourselves feel is real enough. We take what we see personally and we remember it for a long time, sometimes for the rest of our lives. The play serves a catalyst for emotions which lie dormant; and sometimes we need such a catalyst in our work of caring, to set us free from the state of affairs which so easily happens when those in emotional distress ask for help from people whose ruling principle in such cases is to avoid the danger of becoming upset themselves. If we really want to allow people space in which they will feel able to tell their stories, we must somehow learn to do it by the quality of our attention rather than by retreating behind a barrier of 'professionalism' which rules out any possibility of a real meeting of persons. The quality of our attention to the stories people tell us is crucial. In order to arrive where they need to be in the process of re-discovering themselves they need all the help they can get from us. In practice this may simply mean being willing to leave them alone. The idea of allowing someone to 'sort themselves out' may very often be an excuse for simple neglect, although it is more likely to be a reaction to the failure of our attempts to make healing contact with someone it is particularly hard to reach; someone who stubbornly rejects our well-meant offers of comfort and support. It may be of course that we understand very well why they are doing this, but our lack of success in providing 'the answer' is something we tend to take very personally indeed and the idea that they may in some way be in a better position to help themselves than we are to help them suddenly seems very attractive.

(b)   Self-work

It may however turn out to be just what they need. Wounded people need space. The fact that we are troubled by their pain should not allow us to confuse their suffering with our own: not, at least, until they feel ready for us to share their feelings with us. Prospero's island is a place of retreat where anger and hurt are worked through by the people concerned. That is the whole point; it is not what Prospero actually does to his shipwrecked guests which brings about a change in the way they think, feel and behave about themselves and other people, but what they themselves are able to let happen under the special circumstances of their isolation from the wider world. As Alonso put it:

This is as strange a maze as e'er men trod (Act V sc.1)

For us the island may stand as a symbol of the isolation which can be healing insofar as it relieves us of the pressure of other people's attitudes and expectations. On the island, people re-discover themselves, finding out who they really are. In the island setting things about people's character and motives stand out with particular clarity, as living case studies of themselves: Stephano and Trincula are childlike and gullible, Sebastian and Antonio ruthlessly self seeking, old Gonzalo, staunch and loyal, while for Miranda and Ferdinand the island-drama provides the opportunity to re-invent themselves in freely choosing each other. These and so many other things are brought before us and them by the island, to be attended to or ignored as we may see fit. They are there as and for themselves. If we want to find out about them it has to be on their terms.

For many if not most people there will have been times and places which have had a transforming effect on the way they have come to experience being alive. Other people will certainly have contributed to the significance of these changes of direction; they will always be remembered for the part they played in our personal history. The event of change, however, possesses a significance which sets it apart from ordinary life even when it is most extraordinary. These crucial junctions stand outside time and happen in a setting which is all their own. They must be allowed to do so. Certainly, there is a sense in which they make their own space; but our eagerness to put an end to pain by finding a way in which we can stop it happening by operating directly upon it, so that we are not always to co-operate with the instinct which drives emotionally wounded people to seek solitude in which to set about the painful process of healing themselves.

At times in their long history, psychiatric hospitals have functioned in this way for at least some of their more temporary patients. This is no longer seen as an important aspect of healthcare, however. Writing at the end of the last century the Secretary of the British Medical Association had this to say:

> The sad fact is that while we may abhor many of the
> features of the old system of mental hospitals from which
> we have progressed, we still do not have any coherent plan
> to replace them with some kind of 21st century model
> which will provide asylum in a human and domestic
> setting for those patients whose mental illness is either
> recurrently or permanently so severe that life for them in
> the community is intolerable. (Dr. E.M Armstrong: private
> communication)

During the last decades of their existence, the old asylums resumed a role which they had been forced to abandon a century earlier, that of places of short-term refuge where emotionally troubled and traumatised people could find a welcome when the pressures of life became too intense, staying until they themselves felt well enough to leave. At the time there was a good deal of criticism aimed at the 'revolving door' policy, despite its obvious usefulness in keeping serious mental breakdown at bay, but it lessened the hospital's terrifying reputation as a place of permanent incarceration. Here is one person's memory of the hospital in those days:

> Here was treatment, food and shelter
> A space to find your place in
> and that blessed word - Asylum
> Here was a Community, a world

where you might find a welcome
succour and some Peace,
and when the darkness came,
someone to hold
and to be held by. (Ron Ayres)

Places like that are not easy to find. The nearest equivalent nowadays would probably be a retreat house or centre for spiritual healing – so long as the 'spirituality' is not too intensive and the aim is to restore people to themselves and not to make disciples. Wounded people must be allowed to find what they need for themselves and not have it thrust at them by those convinced that they already know the answer.

- I didn't know what I was looking for when I came, and when I found it I didn't know what it was. Or at least I knew but I couldn't explain to anyone else.
- I found all sorts of things about myself. For instance, I never painted anything before I came here and seriously not what I really meant. Some of the things I did I brought back with me. They're on the wall at home. I don't think they're all that good but they mean a lot to me. Most of all they remind me of being there. Being there, and feeling better.

In fact art plays a crucial part in this kind of rediscovery of personal wholeness. It seems that the truthfulness which belongs to things that are imaged forth without being clearly stated is implied by the kind of retreat which is able to heal us in the way we have been describing, 'from the outside in'. Caliban describes how even he is able to be comforted by Prospero's music therapy:

Be not afeard: the isle is full of noises,
Sounds and sweet airs, that give delight,
and hurt not.
Sometimes a thousand twanging instruments
Will hum about mine ears; and sometimes voices,
That if I had wak'd after long sleep
Will make me sleep again. (Act III sc.2)

Wounded lives, traumatically interrupted autobiographies, like broken bodies, take a long time to heal. If anything, they may take longer. Perhaps the clearest example is the trauma of bereavement. Ever since Freud's landmark study of 'grief-work' (Mourning and Melancholia, 1917), psychotherapists have been aware of the intense psychological involvement of mourners in their own processes of healing: This is not something which is undertaken as a project, but a change which is worked through at an unconscious level. There is no conscious determination to ignore what has happened, to 'put the past behind us'. Quite the opposite: to do this would be a way of trying to forget someone whom we may have built our life around, and so to deprive ourselves of even the memory of happiness. For bereaved people to try to forget can feel like insulting someone it is still vitally necessary to keep on the most loving terms with, the beloved custodian of 'the memories which are all I've got now they're gone'. Memory is, and always will be very precious indeed.

What changes in time is the kind of remembering which takes place. As gradually we re-invest in the world which remains around us, the memories which spell only loss and deprivation fall into place as part of our ongoing experience of life, able to comfort us by belonging to the world we are engaged in making our home in, not to shatter that world or stand tragically outside it, but to give it depth and reality. Freud explains that

> In mourning, time is needed for the command of reality-
> testing to be carried out in detail. (1917).

He goes on to say that it is only possible to feel free from the intolerable weight of loss "when this work has been accomplished". It is the bereaved themselves who do this restorative work, for it is only they who can. We, the rest of us, help most when we allow them the space and time to do it.

As with grief, so with other human burdens and afflictions, most if not all of which involve some degree of grief-work. If we want to help – and of course we do – we must learn to do so without either rushing or crowding. We must admit to ourselves that there are some things we cannot put right by taking direct action – and learn how to allow space for renewal. Sometimes states of mind are regarded as evidence of sickness because they do not respond to medical treatment. What is known as 'pathological grief' is a good example of this, as the following case study shows very clearly.

Joe Grice (Aged 60)

Mr Grice's performance at work had been deteriorating and the Social Services Department had been asked to visit his home as it was known that he was living by himself and might be in need of support. Mr Grice spent a great deal of time by himself. The Community Psychiatric Nurse who visited him suspected him of suffering from depression, and the GP prescribed anti-depressive medication. The CPN's account of his visit contains the following:

> Mr Grice produced a bulging wallet containing birth certificates and death certificates plus undertaker's receipts in connection with the burial of both his parents and most of his siblings. He told me that a neighbour of his had accused him of 'living with the dead'. He certainly seemed to want to talk at great length about the various funerals he had attended and been involved in arranging.

It seems that Joe had always been surrounded by a company of relatives and friends, but over the years these had dwindled in number. It was this which he found himself unable to face. The youngest of thirteen children, he was still in some ways the little boy of the family, but of all his siblings only one was still living. This was his sister Eileen, who for a long time had been his main source of companionship. She was a widow, he a bachelor; together they preserved the family identity. Joe's preoccupation in life, and he returned to it continually, concerned the remarriage of his sister. To him the event seemed a personal betrayal; not only did Eileen take a husband, supplanting Joe as the male of the household, she chose someone from the next village, declining to take Joe's advice and marry his own best friend, so keeping things within the friendship network. Finally his resentment got the better of him and he attacked the interloper with a bottle, doing him no serious harm but finally alienating Eileen and causing him banishment from the family home. Things came to a climax when his remaining brother died suddenly, leaving Joe himself alone and unsupported, the huge family's sole survivor.

The CPN noted that

> Mr Grice did not show any particular distress when talked to about his dead relatives but spoke quite conversationally. I got the impression that, although he knew they were dead and he was the sole survivor (apart from Eileen who had placed herself beyond the pale by her marriage), yet in a sense they all live on in the documents in his wallet.

Joe's identity depended on these reminders of his former life. Outside his flat he kept away from social contacts. Persuaded by his CPN to attend depression support at a local Day Hospital, he declined to eat the food provided there: "I want to get back to my own place where I'm in charge of what I eat. I can't get a good sandwich here. I don't know what they're on about. There's nothing wrong with me." At the same time however, he definitely seemed to enjoy the company while he was with the group, entertaining its members with his photographs and artefacts. The group organiser recorded that

> far from being depressed, he was in fact benefiting from the
> social support which his dead family still gave him through
> his memories of the time when he was the favoured member
> of a wide family circle. Because he had distanced himself
> from his sister and her friends, Joe really needed this
> support. His sense of identity depended on it.

Joe's certificates were credentials rather than mementoes; his consuming interest in funerals was not the evidence of a morbid state of mind, but a genuine belief in the enduring solidarity of family ties and their continuance beyond the grave. What had seemed to the CPN to be obsessional behaviour was not in fact the result of the repetitive thought patterns associated with clinical depression, but the search to find a way towards recuperation and reinvestment. As the CPN said, "Joe really needed the presence of the dead to keep him alive."

Joe showed his certificates and photographs to the people he met, despite the alienating effect this had upon his original wide circle of friends. (His doctor noted, "He does not appear to regard belonging as a matter of contractual responsibility to his immediate associates but of membership of an external group which alone can give him protection.") Far from avoiding company he welcomed it, but only on his terms. With the aid of the documented evidence of belonging he laboured to rebuild a world in which to belong. In the words of Pius Ojara, "The sense of loss becomes transformative when we begin, imaginatively and relationally, to reconstruct in new ways the sense of who we are" (2006:238). To do this, we need space in which to move onwards.

CHAPTER 4:
Heirarchies

(a)   The Pecking Order

When people are thrown together on their own resources a degree of organisation is necessary for survival; it is certainly easier to survive with the help of other people, both physically and emotionally, and individuals recognise the need for some kind of systematic arrangement for particular contributions towards the general good. In this necessity for goods and services counts more than personal inclination so far as what Durkheim called "the division of labour" is concerned. Starting from scratch the process is pragmatic, each person making her or his individual contribution to the pursuit of health, wealth and happiness according to his or her ability.

On the theme of islands we might imagine a group of people who find themselves cast away from their previous means of support will set about constructing some kind of temporary social structure, in which practical abilities – hunting and fishing, growing crops, improvising tools, setting broken bones and finding plants which possess healing properties – would be held in higher public esteem than more abstract capabilities. This being the case, they would be likely to see themselves as one or several special groups within the community, a kind of practitioners' in-group.

More important than skill, however, is the imputation of authority which can survive even shipwreck. Those survivors who previously, and in circumstances which were entirely different, occupied positions of esteem, earned or inherited, may now be in a position to assume a social dignity held to be qualitatively different from the mere possession of skill – which after all can be acquired – whereas these folk already possess what is considered to be a much more important and valuable characteristic: the ability to lead. The result of this is a degree of similarity between social arrangements which to begin with looked so excitingly different, such a challenge for finding new ways of doing things together; and these are only two contributions to the emerging social hierarchy. Eventually our univalue society will possess much more than a tradesperson/professional class and an aristocratic/administrative one. It will be a network of interlocking groups, all of them to a degree dependent on the others, a pyramid of responsibility narrowing as it gains authority and social prestige. There is, of course, continual movement both between and within groups as places are exchanged at all levels of the social order; but there is always a need for some kind of overall authority and for organised ways of carrying on the work of the community.

All this is obvious enough. How does it apply to the business of living together on an island, where the setting is new and strange certainly, but the personal histories of the people involved remain just the same – as do their characters, of course. So how does the 'pecking order' of social belonging apply to Prospero's island?

(b)   New World – New Life?

> ...treason, felony,
> Sword, pike or gun, or need of any engine,
> Would I not have; but nature should bring forth
> Of its own kind, all foison, all abundance,
> To feed my innocent people. (Act II sc.1)

Gonzalo describes the perfect commonwealth, the state of affairs he would be pleased to contribute to if he were in charge of the arrangements made for his own and his companions' life on the island where they have been shipwrecked. Antonio and Sebastian, who are of a less altruistic turn of mind, proceed to make fun of him.

This, of course, is not at all surprising: the paradise Gonzalo is describing lies beyond their reach; but Sebastian and Antonio have their own dreams of ways in which the shipwreck can be made use of, but to a more selfish purpose than the one he has described. So far as they are concerned the social arrangements will remain very much the same, simply re-worked to their own advantage. It is a familiar situation, existing wherever people experience a radical interruption in the way that their lives have previously been organised.

The Tempest begins with just such an event as the ship in which the King of Naples and his court has been travelling runs into a terrifying storm and is completely wrecked: "We split, we split, we split!" Splitting takes place not only in timbers but lives, or at least life-stories; and of course, in all the arrangements we make for social living. In the case of Alonso's court the fault line already exists, disguised as two traitorous noblemen who themselves are perpetuating a history of betrayal and consequently anger which lies at the very heart of The Tempest, emerging in the figure of Caliban – Prospero's "poisonous slave" whom some have seen as Prospero's own anger detached to roam the island until his master is able to acknowledge his presence and needs.

Seen from this point of view the island has more in common with the world of Sebastian and Antonio than with Gonzalo's hoped for Utopia. The fact is, of course, that the island contains images and archetypes of both; for Caliban there is Ariel, for Antonio and Sebastian we have Miranda and Ferdinand. As expressed by the people who inhabit it the island is not biased in either direction. It is simply a place for living, a time when people and other kinds of creature find themselves having to learn to live together. Here, on the island, conditions are more difficult than usual, not only because it is an island but because it is this island, which exists in a play and nowhere else – always a heightened form of existence, intentionally so in order to gain our attention to whatever is going on and become imaginatively involved in it.

This chapter is mainly concerned with people's attempts to organise themselves into communities, concentrating on some of the things which interfere with this. Like the rest of the book it takes as its jumping-off point Prospero's Island and the situation of those who find themselves shipwrecked on it. In this case a group of survivors has to find a way of organising themselves for individual security and mutual welfare.

Looking at this kind of situation we might perhaps expect that some social boundaries would perhaps be adjusted or even redrawn altogether. It is easy to imagine that the trauma of shipwreck would have produced a new kind of society altogether as those involved were brought face to face with the need to exist in a world so radically transformed, where none of the old ways of dealing with the business of living exerted its former urgency, or even appeared to have the relevance it once possessed. For instance, is it really necessary under island circumstances to have a butler? Although a jester might certainly come in handy. This is the kind of situation which anthropologists call 'liminal'; in other words it exists in a time and place which does not possess its own stable ways of behaving, having lost the security of one kind of social belonging without having established a new one to any reliable extent. 'Liminal' situations are conditions of 'betweenness' and the people who inhabit them are what Victor Turner calls "threshold people".

Such people do not exist 'outside' society, but in their own special kind of society, possessing its own interpersonal expectations characterised by a heightened regard for tolerance and the inclusion of personal differences. According to Turner,

> The attributes of liminality are necessarily ambiguous since this condition and these persons elude or step through the network of classifications that normally locate states and positions in cultural space. (1974:81)

Those in Alonso's court have lost their footing in the world they knew and had learned to deal with. When they crawl up the beach they have no idea what is waiting for them. Gonzalo urges them to "weigh our sorrow with our comfort". They have at least been saved from death – but for what sort of life? Certainly not one which they are ready to contemplate with any enthusiasm.

This is the kind of situation which is familiar to those who find themselves in liminal situations, and it often gives rise to a radical social re-ordering, characterised by what Turner calls "communitas" in which roles may become dramatically reversed.

> What is interesting about liminal phenomena is the blend they offer of lowliness and sacredness of homogeneity and comradeship. (1974:82)

This, he says, is behaviour associated with initiation into a new position within society, and in some form or other it characterises all human social behaviour, being "a matter of giving recognition to an essential and generic human bond, without which there could be no society" (p.83).

In the case of King Alonso and his household it would be a mistake to look for this behaviour too early. Any relinquishing of social constraints and re-acknowledgement of a common humanity must look for liminality to assert itself more slowly as island magic takes hold of the inhabitants.

The most striking example of role reversal is the task provided for the King of Naples' son, who must demonstrate his love for Prospero's daughter by becoming a lumberjack; but the crucial reversal of status must wait for its proper place, at the turning point of the play's action, where Alonso and his courtiers are stripped of their dignity and reduced to despised outcasts. Ariel sums up their new status, or lack of it:

> You are three men of sin, whom Destiny,
> That hath to instrument this lower world
> And what is in't, the never-surfeited sea
> Hath caused to belch up you; and on this island
> Where man doth not inhabit; you 'mongst men
> Being most unfit to live. I have made you mad;
> And even with such-like valour men hang and drown
> Their proper selves. (Act II sc.3)

On this experience of total disintegration of current authority structures Prospero's future society will depend. Social arrangements must be, and be seen to be, temporary and open to radical reversal. The main theme of the play is mirrored in the antics of the clowns, thus demonstrating how futile the search for status and position really is:

> "Trinculo, the King and all our company else being
> drown'd, we will inherit here. Here, bear my bottle."
> (Act II sc.2)

It would also be misleading to expect too great a change in social arrangements as a result of the island experience. There will still be a King of Naples, and it will still be Alonso – only now he will have the king's son as his son-in-law. Relationships will have changed but not society itself. Even a shipwreck has not managed as much as that. Nor, of course, was it actually intended to do. The island has an essentially limited purpose. Basically it is a personal one, involving Prospero and his perfidious brother Antonio and the outstanding need to set matters straight between them. The purpose was certainly not to bring about any kind of revolution in the structure of society. Social roles are definitely to be respected and preserved, so that they may be returned to or retained by their rightful owners. Coming ashore from the shipwreck, Gonzalo draws attention to the fact that the survivors' clothing remains unaffected:

> our garments, being, as they were, drench'd in the sea,
> hold, notwithstanding, their freshness and glosses, being

rather new-dy'd, than stain'd with salt water. (Act II sc.1)

His companions remain unimpressed, presuming no doubt that the preservation of these marks of rank is perfectly natural and a sign of God's investment in the status quo (in fact the same thing has happened to the ship's crew; Prospero is determined to start his experiment with a clean sheet, avoiding unnecessary and undeserved suffering.)

There is another reason why the kind of egalitarianism associated with initiations appears not to have taken hold in this case, and that is that an opposite and balancing principle is at work here, that governing the organisation of groups within society itself. People want to be confident that they are part of a relationship or group that gives them meaning and security. The need to belong is, as Twinge and Baumeister have reminded us, "fundamental to human life" (2005:4). In structured societies, wherever people make arrangements for living together on a permanent or semi-permanent basis, personal identity is assessed according to the degree of definition attached to the position a person takes up within the social hierarchy or chain of social importance. People think more highly of themselves if they are able to see themselves as making progress towards a more powerful or influential position within society than the one they currently hold; and as psychologists point out, our relationship with ourselves largely governs the way in which we regard other people, and consequently treat them.

The obvious result of this is a tendency on the part of those who feel sure of their place within society or their membership of a particular social group to feel less threatened by outsiders than those who do not; particularly outsiders who aim to change their status and become insiders. A group with boundaries which have become too flexible, whose outline has lost its definition – i.e. its identity – is as threatening to those who see their security in group membership as one which has no barriers at all, so that it can no longer function as a group at all. Left to themselves, human groups tend to proliferate as the human urge to belong in an exclusive way causes the structures to reproduce themselves. Those who, for one reason or another fail to qualify for a group to which they aspire form a corresponding group of excluded people which sooner or later itself assumes exclusiveness so that other individuals find themselves rejected and proceed to look around themselves for allies. In this way 'in-groups' create 'out-groups' in order for those to become 'in-groups' and so on. This process is almost a cliché of social psychology, as indeed it must be if it describes something so very basic: the need to belong to a group of other people and to form such groups if none are available. Even those who usually regard themselves to be self sufficient 'loners' have a tendency to talk about themselves as if they were members of a company of private people to be found everywhere: "people like us", in fact. Some human groups are more public than others which exist only in abstraction, but the operation of including something or someone as the member of a group belongs to that of taking thought.

The need for individuals to attach themselves to others in this generic way certainly goes back a long way. Certainly it would be hard to think of the biological family as this kind of group – although relationships formed during the first months and years of life certainly affect the ease with which we are able to make them later on. Writing from the psychoanalytic point of view, Erik Erikson identifies the period of most intense awareness of peer group activity as lasting from the beginning of school age to the end of adolescence. During this time the need to join and form groups contributes powerfully to an individual's sense of being a person to the extent that individuals are likely to describe themselves as a member of this or that important group of other people. This is the stage in life which begins with gang membership and culminates in fraternity and sorority enthusiasms; after this the need begins to decrease, although the tendency to turn to groups of other like-minded people for support and encouragement never really goes away; if it did, of course, any kind of social organisation would be impossible.

Later stages of development do, however, make this kind of social formation more problematical. Erikson point out that

> Young adults emerging from the adolescent search for a
> sense of identity [outside the group, that is] can be eager
> and willing to fuse their identities in mutual intimacy and
> to share them with individuals who, in work, sexuality
> and friendship promise to prove complementary ... The
> psychosocial antithesis to intimacy, however, is isolation, a
> fear of remaining separate and unrecognised. (1985:70)

He comments that

> the greatest danger of isolation is a regressive and hostile
> returning of the identity conflict, a fixation in the earliest
> conflict with the primal Other.

Erikson traces this need to avoid isolation and yet not be totally subsumed and lose identity back to the very earliest stages of over-conscious self-hood. It is certainly well established, so that its frustration tends to result in behaviour which is considered, often with good cause, to be antisocial. Yet again this kind of aggressive reaction turns out to be a form of pro-social behaviour in that its aim is the discovery of another set of alliances, a new group in fact. "Although definite evidence is not available," say Twinge and Baumeister, "it seems plausible that socially excluded individuals become anti-social because they no longer see the point in being pro-social." (Abram, Hogg and Marques 2005:32) This does not mean that they no longer want or need to belong alongside other people, but simply that the society which rejects them is, in some way or another, superseded by another with a more restricted – and probably even more exclusive – membership which may be the reason why those rejected by the wider society show an equal or even greater degree of self-respect than those who remain acceptable.

> People strongly desire social attachments, exert considerable energy to develop and sustain them, and are adversely affected by their dissolution or absence. The need to belong may be evolutionary adaptive. (Major and Eccleston; in Abram, Hogg and Marques 2005:63)

Belonging by itself is not enough, however. The circumstances of belonging are very important and may even be crucial to whether or not it is worthwhile to continue membership. Groups which are characterised by a hierarchical rather than a democratic structure may have strict rules about the influence various grades of belonging may exert on the private and public life of the group. If one's position within a group makes it impossible or very difficult to identify one's own feelings and attitudes with those of the group as a whole, one may wish to switch groups; or if, for practical reasons such a thing is impossible, to carve out a new allegiance within the wider framework of the group as a whole. This, of course, is what happens at the various authority levels within organization in which different kinds of job responsibility provide opportunities for localised expressions of the exclusiveness which results in the formation of groups. Thus the division of labour necessary from an institutional standpoint, economic or otherwise, gives birth to a succession of groups-within-groups: political, religious, commercial, social, therapeutic, each marked by a degree of defensiveness originating in the human need to belong without being excluded, ignored or swallowed whole.

All this may go somewhere towards explaining why, even though shipwrecked into an initiatory scenario of the kind associated with the access of "homogeneity and comradeship", the shipwrecked court still retains its customary social configuration. Admittedly the kind of structural collapse which marks the liminal phase at the centre of the process of ritual transformation has not yet actually arrived on the scene at this point. When it does, though, social categories will remain the same: there will be a king, a duke, an ex-duke, lords and servants, just as there were in Act I.

This does not mean, however, that there has been no movement in the sub-groups which make up the larger system. It appears that the trauma of the shipwreck and the sense of a hiatus in the course of ordinary life has opened up an opportunity for Antonio to take an important step towards group leadership by working on Sebastian's own greed for power in order to enlist him in his plan for yet another re-ordering of the political scene; this time more Draconian still. Sebastian does not need much persuasion:

Thy case, dear friend,
Shall be my precedent; as thou got'st Milan,
I'll come by Naples. (Act II sc.1)

Even more typical than a conspiracy among high-born traitors, however, is the alliance formed by Stephano and Trinculo, both of them domestic servants whose skills are likely to be used but not socially valued, with Prospero's servant-monster Caliban. "Seeking inclusion by others who are similarly stigmatised is likely" say Major and Eccleston "to have a number of psychological benefits." (2005:76) The benefit certainly seems to be mutual. Of all the shipwrecked survivors Trinculo and Stephano are the most disreputable, having lost any evidence of respectability they may have once possessed; Caliban, on the other hand, is the archetype of social stigma, an outcast by birth and ancestry, occupation and personality. He catches sight of a bottle and recognises fellow creatures infinitely more congenial than any he has known before and offers the service which is his nature and function:

I'll swear upon that botte to be thy true subject, for the
liquor is not earthly.

So he transfers his allegiance: Stephano with his bottle is now King, not Prospero with his staff – until, at the end of the play they are once more brought face to face, of course.

This kind of group belonging, the membership of recognisable sub-groups within the overall organizations of society or a large organization, lies at the root of all our behaviour together, whether or not we actually live on islands. Human beings, as we have seen, function as social animals; they depend on others for their own self-realisation and try to form close personal relationships with a relatively small group of people whom they regard as comprising their own particular world. Large group membership is beneficial but on the whole small group interaction is preferred as providing actual face-to-face contact with another individual. The durability of such groups is considerable. When in abnormal circumstances they are disrupted, they tend to return to their former state once such circumstances cease to exist. This fact stands out clearly in The Tempest which is its own world of relationships tough enough to withstand life-changing experiences and still preserve the social order. (It is worth noting that the same thing happens in J.M. Barrie's play about socially privileged people shipwrecked on an island, The Admirable Crichton.)

(c)   Stigma

The other outstanding social message very definitely concerns stigma, the situation in which individuals and groups experience social exclusion on the part of sections of society or of society as a whole. The underlying dynamic stands out clearly as the formation of groups involves the exclusion of individuals who are not considered to be qualified for membership; and if the excluded individuals form themselves reactively into their own group, this will be by definition of lower status than the excluding one. The system requires that even if group members move to another group, the relative position of groups remains stable; some will be higher, others lower, and the higher will be harder to join. Indeed the stability of the system as a source of authority requires that dominant groups should be out of reach of all but a very few. This, of course, is what makes Stephano's pretensions so absurd, so that it is not simply being drunk which makes him laughable. It seems comic to us that a butler should indulge fantasies about being a king, but it is only funny because it is absurd – absurdly impossible. In fact Stephano and his two companions are shipwrecked by the entrenched power of stigma, as it affects those of us watching the play in our reaction to people like that as well as other personages on stage who are obviously more socially acceptable. One of the things plays set out to do is to bring home the universal nature of unacknowledged human attitudes towards other people. Stigmatisation of some kind or another appears to be an important factor in any kind of social organization, and thus to play a part in the way we gain a sense of belonging on which personal identity depends. Hogg, Fielding and Darley put this in an even starker way by claiming that

> subjective rejection of deviates is a mechanism that allows
> group members to maintain certainty about the validity
> of in-group standards and thus the superiority of group
> identity. (2006:196)

Understandable though its workings may be, its effects can be devastating. People who feel that they are stigmatised are psychologically wounded in a way which can leave them permanently scarred. Because the harm has been inflicted in the part of their awareness specifically concerned with others' perception of them, the need to hide or even to run away begins to exert increasing pressure:

- the more other people know about me, the harder it is to just be me. I feel everyone just sees me as 'one of those'.
- they advised me not to let anyone know I'd been in a psychiatric hospital. Don't tell them where you've been for the last couple of months or you won't get a job. They were right; when I did mention it at an interview you could see their faces change.
- I never tell people which road I live in or even the name of the estate – that would be worse – I just tell them the area. After all, there's all kinds of people in the area.

An HIV positive woman, a 'user of psychiatric services' and someone unfortunate enough to have been born in the wrong part of town: these are three examples out of millions that could have been chosen. Social stigma is a way of feeling better by making someone else feel worse, in which the power to harm is out of all proportion to the satisfaction gained. Erving Goffman describes stigmatised people as suffering from "spoiled identity". Stigmatisation, he says, renders people "not quite human" (1968:17). Almost anybody can be the victim of stigma because almost anything may be seized upon as a reason for it. It is a way of keeping one's own fears and anxieties away from oneself by projecting them on people whom one hopes never to have to meet in the flesh: classes and groups of people who have come into direct contact with the condition or way of behaving which is shunned, whatever this may be. This is why stigmatised people feel soiled, not by the things for which they are excluded, but by the action of exclusion itself, which leaves an invisible taint on personal identity which affects the way in which the victim sees life as a whole. Nothing in life so affects our experience of life; nothing demonstrates so clearly the power and scope of social pressure. In primitive societies the force of social rejection was enough to make individuals fall ill and die. Robert Kastenbaum has described how "A person is socially dead when there is an absence of those behaviours that we would expect to be directed towards a living person" (1969:15) . In the awareness of some stigmatised individuals, to be excluded from the social group to which they aspire and believe they should by rights belong, is a death sentence itself; or would be if it were not for the support of others in the same situation as themselves.

Those involved in pastoral care are very likely to come into contact with individuals who are suffering the depersonalising effect of stigma, either on their own or through membership of stigmatised sections of society. Because their state of mind reflects a social reality, part of the way communities are organised in order to feel authentic themselves, treating them as if they have a psychological problem which is responsible for their condition is not an effective way of helping them. It is after all what they are usually told! ('Your feelings are delusional, no-one really thinks that about you'; 'you have an obsessional personality.') There may well be some truth in such judgements, but they are by no means the whole story, and attempting to tie someone's anxieties down by giving them a convenient psychiatric label does not help, because it is an attempt to distance the person concerned from a responsibility which they already recognise as not being theirs in any case. Saying 'Don't worry, it's not your fault; it's an illness' is no good for them at all – they know it isn't their fault; they would really prefer that it was so that they could do something about it.

Because stigma is a by-product of social formation, caused by the way in which communities themselves come into being, it does not easily respond to therapeutic approaches designed to deal with abnormal psychological conditions. At some point in the common life of our island, the one we are imagining in this book, some will feel socially excluded: a quality, tendency, economic or hereditary condition will be attributed to them which makes it impossible for them to belong in a particular social group – or any group at all other than the one to which they are confined by their condition as 'outsiders'.

The circumstances of human social life being what they are, most people will themselves have been the victim of this kind of exclusion. Only at its most extreme however does it result in actual stigmatisation of individuals and groups. Excluded people feel angry at being excluded. Exclusion itself does not constitute stigmatisation, only the imputation of an essential inferiority – an inferior way of being human. This is the wound which creates such intense resentment, because it is both undeserved and ineradicable. "If you have a stigma you only have yourself to blame, although it isn't your fault." You can only blame yourself because others have projected their own terror of not belonging on to you, and you appear to have no option other than to accept their judgement.

Pastoral care is concerned with people who have chronic feelings that they are victims of stigmatisation, whether or not the carer feels that they have any reason for feeling this way. They need what Personal Construct Psychology calls "the credulous approach" (1991:241) if only because not to believe their story is to be open to the charge of stigmatisation oneself. The aim here is self-expression with a view to the safe release of anger, an ambiguous anger directed at the self for being excluded, as well as the individuals or groups cast in a stigma-inducing role. Kelly reminds us that people who ask us for help with their emotional difficulties are always "like the proverbial customer, always right." Their version of the state of affairs possesses a valuable truthfulness about the way they themselves see the situation which should never be discounted. After all, they may be right; and so far as they are concerned, they are right:

> This is not to say that the client always describes events in
> the way other people would describe them, or in the way it
> is commonly agreed that they did happen. (1991:241)

People who say they are victims of social prejudice which causes them to feel stigmatised characteristically have their own view of things. Those setting out to care for them pastorally should be willing to listen to what they have to say, and to grant them the opportunity to be believed.

On Prospero's island both servants and lords obey the rules of social stratification and are consequently open to feeling their pinch. Nobody, however, is more excluded than Caliban, Prospero's monstrous slave, who feels and is deprived of any rights of citizenship whatsoever. He has, in fact, been created for stigma, his very being a warning about what life could be like and a sharp reminder to others to count their blessings. Caliban really has been kept permanently in a subservient position and deprived of any way of escape by the only way his nature would have allowed him, which would have been by mating with the only available female, Miranda:

> Oh ho, Oho! woud't have been done!

Thou dids't prevent me; I had peopled else
This isle with Calibans. (Act I sc.2)

Caliban is at the bottom of the pile. No-one knows it better than he does. Indeed, he spends most of the play complaining about it and about his inability to escape his master's ill will towards him, which he, of course, sees as completely undeserved: "I must obey, his art is of such power ..." One of the things which causes Caliban such grief and pain is the absence of anyone who will or can show him any sympathy, or at least try to understand his position. He moans to Prospero:

You taught me language, and my profit on't
Is, I know how to curse. (Act I sc.2)

Watching the play we may assume that many stigmatised people feel the same about the society in which they themselves live.

CHAPTER 5
Laboratories For Living

(a)   Belonging Together

Lindisfarne, also known as Holy Island, is an island off the coast of Northumberland. It is joined to the mainland by a causeway more than a mile long which, at high tide, is submerged, cutting off the island completely – making it an island, in fact. During high season at the times of day when the causeway is able to be used, Lindisfarne buzzes with activity as tourists roam across it to visit the castle and ruined abbey and to buy souvenirs of St Cuthbert and St Aidan; and then suddenly, when the tide starts to come in again, lapping at the edges of the causeway, everything goes silent, just like it was before the cars and tourist buses arrived. Lindisfarne is peaceful with the longed for tranquillity which brought the visitors here and which is only present when they are not ...

But this is misleading. During these peaceful intermissions the island is actually a hive of activity as the islanders get on with the business of living, of being the people of Lindisfarne at work on their own and one another's lives. Its quietness is the concentration of work – and play – in progress. It is a focused peacefulness, a kind of awareness of the underlying purpose of engaging with reality. Strange though it may at first seem, it is the quality of mindfulness associated with children's games – involvement without anxiety. Writing this I'm extremely conscious that someone who actually lives on Holy Island is likely to have a very different view about what happens 'between-times' on their island; nevertheless to an observer there is a very powerful contrast between the intense commercial activity – the essence of goal-centredness – and the reflexive moment when the island draws breath and turns again to other things. Compared with tourism and its ancillary activities, this certainly represents living in the moment, something which we normally associate with artistic experience and non-competitive playing of all kinds. Social psychologists distinguish between motivation which is intrinsic – that is, coming from within the subject – and that which is extrinsic and dictated by the pressures of life.

But life's pressures demand relief, and times of extrinsic involvement need to be balanced by times of relaxation. The community life of the island corresponds to group experience of all kinds, which can be serious or frivolous, hilarious or sombre and intense, and is probably all these things by turns. This chapter is mainly concerned with groups – and islands – as laboratories for living, and with the corporate gesture of space-making as the group establishes its own territory, the place and time in which it will operate. This need not be only one place, one occasion, although times often vary more considerably than settings. Wherever the group meets is the group's own world, a fact which the world wide web demonstrates extremely efficiently. Groups are ways of relating to others; they are states of mind, not times and places, but because of the agreement which binds them together they carry with them a notion of 'group territoriality'.

The word 'agreement' should, of course, be used cautiously. It refers to a willingness to participate, not an undertaking to be all of the same mind. Far from it: group membership carries with it the freedom to argue and to arrive at minority conclusions; or at least, any group which aims at being of emotional and intellectual benefit to its members will be founded on this principle of freedom to be oneself. However, as Bion pointed out, this is not an easy thing to achieve:

> All groups stimulate and at the same time frustrate the
> individuals composing them; for the individual is impelled
> to seek the satisfaction of his needs in his group and is at
> the same time inhibited in this aim by the primitive fears
> that the group arouses. (1961:188)

This is the dynamism which enables groups to be creative, the dialectic which seeks an experience of togetherness in which differences are explored and used.

Exploration is an important component within the experience of groups. It is not only states of mind which are investigated and shared, but actual events occurring in the lives of those taking part. This is often done in the form of games, whose serious purpose is both concealed and also exposed by their apparent lack of relevance to 'real life' situations. For example, here are two group games which relate to the 'real life' situation we have been looking at in Lindisfarne. Neither of them is essentially competitive, although both can be made to appear so. In themselves, however, they are exercises in group exploration.

- Whodunit

  Someone arranges furniture and objects within the available space, inviting group members to imagine a scenario which has recently taken place in it: "What do you think has been going on here?"

- Waiter, Waiter

  The group is having dinner in a restaurant. Members take on the role of waiter, maitre d'hotel, chef, hat-check girl etc. The scene is played through from arrival to departure. Next it is repeated in different modes – fast, slow, anxious, very relaxed – finishing by playing the entire scene in reverse (although this is an optional extra).

Again, these are group explorations of situations and people, their differences and similarities. They are exercises in imaginative sharing of a fundamental human experience, that of exploration directed towards discovery. As such they create their own kind of space – the invisible space which they need for their sort of exploration which requires concentration and co-operation, a willingness to disengage from one way of paying attention to whatever is going on within the group in order to join in the shared business of becoming co-creators of something new. This does not mean quitting the real world, simply standing back from it – something we are all quite used to doing by ourselves countless times every day. Now, however, we agree to do it together, each contributing her or his own imaginative reality in a gesture of creative imagination. The co-operation is real in every sense of the word, and the imaginary world created is its excuse. The reality of the group's existence as a group, its shared identity, justifies the 'escape into fantasy' We might argue – and some have done

– that this is what fantasy is really for, to be shared in order to become social reality.

Bertolt Brecht, the playwright whose influence has dominated western theatre for three-quarters of a century, would certainly have thought so. Theatre-space is real because it gives rise to social reality, to allowing ways of organising the business of living. It is a dedicated space, used to bring to life truths about being human which 'need to be seen to be believed'. It is safe space because the reality it presents and projects is a provisional one, so that we can take it or leave it; it is specially focused space, able to capture and hold our attention so that here more than anywhere else we can 'keep to the point' (1964).

It is also intensely personal space. The fact that it is safe allows us to take it personally. This is actually the most important thing about it, as Aristotle pointed out so many centuries ago. Because it is safe and personal, being about people like ourselves in situations to which we are able to relate, it is actually free space. It is free in two ways: first because, being focused, it is detached from the contingencies of our own actual lives; second because we are not forced to take it personally, and this humanises it for us. We can opt out of this experience at any time. We do not have to leave the group – or the theatre – to do so; and of course, if we choose to 'suspend our disbelief' and get involved, then we may have a wholly personal, or even transpersonal, sense of contributing to the action.

We should not be surprised, then, that group work often makes use of dramatic structure. It may use games and improvised play to do so; at a deeper level it uses its own identity, giving dramatic shape and meaning to the stories by those taking part, and to its own story as a group. This is something which we all do with our lives, organising them into so many beginnings and endings to be regarded as episodes in a more extended narrative. The group does the same thing with the life it shares as a group. It uses dramatic distance, the action of standing back from life in order to look at it more closely and to register the degree to which it is itself a social construct – and also in order to create a space in which to do at least a part of one's own living.

(b)   Relational Space – intangible, invisible, without extension, yet possessing a deep personal reality. Through drama of several kinds this betweenness becomes memorably present, helping us explore relationship from the inside by living the process of investigating it. It lies at the very heart of drama's power to refresh and renew, leading us away from preoccupation with ourselves, our own obsessive psychological involvement with ways in which we can, somehow or other, manage to deal with the situations we find ourselves in by controlling our thoughts and feelings according to a system of divide and rule. Drama is an holistic experience, encouraging a state of mind which might be described as 'mindfulness' wherein we are aware not of gaps to be filled but presences to be enjoyed. This is reflection of a different kind, experiential rather than analytical. Certainly there is a place for analysing a play's meaning, but this happens after the curtain has fallen (Grainger 1990). During the action we are part of what is going on, saved from having to make sense of things by the detachment which enables us to let ourselves become engaged with them.

Salvo Petruzzella describes the therapeutic effect of encouraging this kind of awareness within groups:

> The first part ... is set around playing with the elements of drama: tools (body, voice, speech; objects) and structures (the 'as if' frame, narrative and roles). It is what Carl Rogers defined as 'the ability to amuse oneself with elements and concepts' ... It is important because it shapes this particular attitude to experience ...

Later on, however, the 'game' becomes more serious. Pitruzzella describes how its apparent randomness gives rise to more crystallised experience:

> The dramatic process ... is not a progressively accumulative process, but is rather punctuated by special moments which mark discontinuities and qualitative leaps ... During these moments it almost seems that a multitude of fragments scattered along the way ... suddenly take on a visible form, often in the shape of symbolic structures.

Even this, however, is not the climax of the experience of dramatic exploration, for

> the event itself always occurs as a sudden epiphany, engendering surprise and wonder in the therapist too (Pitruzzella, 2000).

It is this sense of wonder which can make dramatherapy memorable, a totally unforgettable experience; but it is not the ideas involved which strike home so powerfully, but the fact of discovery. What it was that was discovered may be hard to put into words:

- It was something about being alive. I can remember the 'when' and 'where' of it but not the 'how'. Not even the 'what' as a matter of fact.
- Don't ask me what we actually did or said. If you want to know, come along and find out …
- I don't know what we do, except that we play a game at some point, usually towards the beginning, before we get started. Then we go a lot deeper, you know?

This *indescribability* of the event is not something confined to dramatherapy, however; in fact it belongs to group work of many kinds. It belongs to the experience of becoming aware of the real presence of other people – their presence, not our ideas about them. The times when it happens are easy to remember. In fact they are difficult to forget, perhaps because they are hard to assimilate cognitively because of the way they are communicated. It is in fact a matter of communication, ideas shared not so much in the form of propositions or statements but as presence. The experience of the group is one of *focused presence*; instead of concentrating on one kind of message, listening hard in order to register precisely what is being said and who is saying it, group members are conscious of another kind of knowing, by participating and mutual recognition not, in the first place, by analysis. As the member of a group, an individual's way of knowing is characteristically global as opposed to unitary, as in groups we focus on being together. The experience is one of diffused encounter interspersed with times of reflection in which we make a more or less conscious decision to withdraw from whatever is going on around – and involving – us in order to make space for recollection. In groups the movement backwards and forwards between 'I-Thou' and 'I-It' is more definite than we aware of its being in face-to-face situations. Psychodynamic psychologists recognise an unconscious level of sharing in which connections made with key figures in our early development are distributed around the group – a 'shared transference' experience, allowing opportunities for the transformation of long-established emotional connections – psychic memories – and the formation of new, more ego-directed linkages.

Carl Rogers is even more explicitly in favour of group experience as a jumping off place for individual freedom. Speaking of what he calls "group process" he describes ways in which groups are able to be aware of things which are beyond our grasp as individuals:

Trust the group process, let it go on. In the group we're
wiser than we know. (Video counselling seminar, Illinois
University, 1973)

This, in fact, is the basis for what may be called group spirituality –
"what it is that makes a group able to communicate with itself in ways
that defy analysis" (Grainger 2003:13). If groups are places of discovery
learning, healing of personal wounds, it is because of the spirituality
which they possess; or rather, which blows through them. The following
is an extract from a group member's attempt to tie the experience down
so that others may understand what she herself has so much difficulty in
communicating in written form:

> I'm writing about something I have difficulty in grasping,
> perhaps because *it* has grasped *me*. I can think of several
> aspects of the experience:
>
> (a) **support**. It's a place where I feel encouraged to express
> myself. I can take chances here I couldn't do anywhere else.
>
> (b) **freedom**. I can relax from all the pressure of the things
> which usually crowd in on me, because this is what the
> group is for – being a group, not just a person on your own,
> so
>
> (c) **learning**; particularly self-learning, learning about
> myself. There are things I didn't know about myself, the
> kind of person I am. Some quite surprising things, in fact,
> so that I find myself coming out with all kinds of stuff.
> Sometimes I surprise myself; once or twice I've got into
> trouble because my frankness has upset other people in the
> group. So –
>
> (d) **awareness of other people**. Sometimes I've said the first
> thing that came into my head and the reaction was hard
> to take. It felt as though everyone turned on me at once.
> Perhaps I touched on something which people find they
> themselves all felt touchy about. Perhaps I was too eager to
> be spontaneous and express myself. (Perhaps I went too far
> in the direction of (a).)
>
> (e) **trust** in the group, because even during these difficult

moments they still managed to hang on in with me so we were able to work through the bad patch. (I realise now that I wasn't the only one that this happened to; perhaps it happened to others and I didn't register, being too keen to 'go with the flow'!) So that –

(f) self-understanding and **self-acceptance**. These two go together as gradually during my time as a group member I found them coming together for me. I really think I know myself better now than I did. I have more compassion for myself and yet I'm more aware of the effect I may sometimes have on other people, so I'm maybe a bit more tolerant about the effect they have on me.

Altogether, a learning experience ...

This woman's testimony bears out the part played by group experiences in achieving the goal of psychotherapy as described by Rogers – that of enabling someone to be "that self which one truly is" – a self only established in personal encounter:

> The expression of self by some members of the group has made it very clear that a deeper and more basic encounter is possible, and the group appears to strive instinctively and unconsciously towards this goal ... Group members move towards becoming more spontaneous, flexible, closely related to their feelings, open to their experience, and closer and more expressively intimate in their interpersonal relationships. (1967)[1]Note

Group members "strive" because they are becoming increasingly conscious of the benefits for the business of living of having discovered more about themselves and the terms and conditions of their own and other people's personhood. This is a movement which is characteristic of the human species, it seems. The instinct referred to is that of 'self-realisation' through exploration. In other words it is, humanly speaking, our curiosity as much as any unconscious force which drives us to know ourselves better – or if it is unconscious then it expresses itself in a very cognitive way as a reasoned intention to find out what makes us behave in particular ways – particularly ways which seem 'unadaptive' and could well be abandoned and replaced, or at least readjusted in order to make a better 'fit'.

1   See also Grainger, 2003.

Above all, human groups are sources of information. They may have an expressive purpose, but the cathartic release of feelings is employed here as a very definite way of making sense: what is this feeling about? What, psychologically speaking, is it for? Most important of all, what role does it play in the way we learn to live with one another in the social situations in which we find ourselves? Groups remind us of the social nature of our most personal feelings and ideas. From this point of view they have more to do with Durkheim than with Freud – or at least with the self-referential model of the human psyche with which he has become associated. The spiritual quality of group experience is totally opposed to any investigation of human processes which regards people as separate organisms detached from their social belonging for the purpose of analysis. Certainly there is room for the kind of focused investigation carried out by scientists, but not under the conditions which they impose on themselves and us. The need to find things out as efficiently as possible and not to be distracted by seeming irrelevancies or ideas about reality which are not really tested but simply taken on trust, belongs to group work as much as to any other kind of serious investigative process; the difference lies in the experimental context, the type of laboratory used.

The group work laboratory is the group itself, in its identity as a group rather than a number of separate individuals. There are, of course, individual members, but the subject of the investigation, agreed on by all taking part, is the nature and quality of their association and its effect on each person's experience of living and dying. This choice of laboratory, one made up of people and their intentions towards one another and not simply a frame for studying objects in, changes the whole nature of the enterprise by acknowledging the presence, within the experiment, of an unseen reality which 'comes with the group' and cannot be distinguished from it. Groups can only be studied as holisms, phenomena whose overall reality exceeds the sum total of their component parts, however we may decide to distinguish these from one another. It would be wrong, however, to assume that conclusions may not be drawn from the work carried out in this kind of laboratory, so long as we are willing to acknowledge the unknowable foundation of our knowing – what it is that made us a group in the first place. Both psychology and sociology give the impression that they are able to tie this down by referring to it as 'instinctual' – a category which is unanalysable by definition; the fact remains that group members experience it as something very different, and it is this different kind of experience which opens the door to a richer understanding of self and other. We have referred to it in language that has not been overtly spiritual, calling it 'relationship', 'betweenness' and 'belonging'. Here in the group context its spirituality is clearly revealed as the intensity of individual confrontation is spread out among those taking part and the sustaining transcendence shines through the whole, giving birth to realistic understandings and creative ideas which make the most ordinary kind of sense.

People who seek the experience of belonging to a group rediscover a particular aspect of their lives which life itself has got in the way of: the conscious search for personal meaning. There is the possibility here in the group for more than advice about dealing with immediate problems, even though that may be forthcoming. At its most characteristic the group symbolises the search for transcendence, the knowledge which lies on the other side of question-and-answer. This means that it is in fact end-less in the sense of not having an achievable purpose. 'Closure' is not enough to satisfy this unspoken agenda; we hunger for what we cannot fully contain.

This is the group experienced and acknowledged as spiritual symbol, rooted in our longing for the beyondness which gives meaning to our movement in time, so that we can perceive the things which happen to us not as any kind of impersonal random succession of events but as real stages of our journey through life. In Paul Ricoeur's words, "The symbol gives rise to thought." (Gunn 1971) What we know of ourselves as group members is inspired by what we do not and cannot know. The knowledge acquired in a group context is the most basic human understanding that, to use Charles Williams' immortal formulation, "salvation lies everywhere in interchange" (1937:248).

The group itself is the symbol; the thoughts to which it gives rise constitute discoveries made about how groups actually function in ways which preserve their own unique identities, as members assume roles within the group structure which have been vacated, temporarily or permanently, by other members. The self-regulatory process serves to maintain the corporate personhood as possessing an identity in its own right and not simply an ad hoc collection of individuals. Once this identity has been acknowledged the group assumes the assertive individuality shown by people who feel sure of themselves. Such a group has the courage to stand on its own feet as an entity possessing what Kurt Lewin described as "the structured properties of a given whole" (quoted in Perls, Hefferline and Goodman 1973:326), in this case a very personal whole indeed. Seen like this, groups are personal in a way which distinguishes them from those who constitute them. They are active symbols of the mystery which is human relationship. In the group symbol we encounter one another in terms of sameness and difference, in Levinas's words

> We recognise the other as resembling us but exterior to
> us; the relationship with the other is a relationship with a
> mystery. (1987:75)

If our search is for mystery we need look no farther than the focused relationship of personhood presented by a group of people who recognise themselves in and by their belonging together in such a way.

(c)   Space for Story

The group is both a story and a presenter of individual stories. In my experience group members are themselves conscious of various stages of a group's ongoing life which invite being arranged into the form of some kind of narrative. As the group learns about the terms of its own belonging together it constructs a story about itself in order to establish an identity by registering ways in which it is unique. Here again drama provides a framework:

> We'd been meeting for some time, but I don't think we
> were really a group until things came to a head and ––
> walked out. Actually they came back later on, but not for a
> couple of sessions, by which time it was different. Actually
> it was their coming back which made it different, although
> things had already begun to change ... But it was the walk-
> out which really made the difference. For a time we thought
> it was all over and things had fallen apart for ever.

By the time it has reached the form recorded above, the account is already a fully fledged story, with a beginning, a middle and an end arranged around a central event, something which seemed like an ending but turned out to be a new beginning. This is the story of the group, one which when shared with other group members was immediately recognised by them as such. During the course of their meeting together every member has, in one way or another, directly or indirectly told her or his story – and their stories have been listened to, so that in line with the way this process works they have become parts of the group's organising narrative while at the same time using it to establish their own integrity and realism. Sometimes the group's meta-narrative modifies the tale told by the individual; sometimes it may corroborate the conclusions he or she draws. Perhaps because the social nature of the group's experience tends towards the optimistic, or at least a positive denouement for the problems and hardships encountered on the way, an individual member may find themselves encouraged to adjust the story they are accustomed to tell themselves and others about themselves. In this way the literary and dramatic genre may change, away from the direction of tragedy towards that of romance or even comedy.

To think in this way at all and particularly to share one's thoughts with others is, of course, a hopeful action in itself. Creativity of any kind is an assertion of the possibility of some kind of meaning. Who can write a genuinely cheerful letter when they are feeling depressed? Yet even the expression of hopelessness is comparatively positive; as Edgar puts it: the worst is not

> As long as we can say 'This is the worst'. (King Lear, Act IV sc.1)
> (He then goes on to transform Gloucester's tragic life story with a powerfully presented piece of therapeutic drama.)

Pastoral care makes extensive use of personal narrative. According to Willows and Swinton:

> listening to and telling stories lies at the heart of all human experience and forms part of the fabric of the practical theological task. We locate ourselves in the world, know who we are, where we have been and where we are going in and through the stories we tell about ourselves and through the 'meta-narratives' by which we choose to live. Formative experiences, for example, such as suffering, alienation, chaos and confusion, are invariably communicated and interpreted through the stories that people tell about themselves and their experiences.

– and they add that:

> Moreover it could be argued that the essence of faith itself has to do with the possibility of encountering stories that transform who we are and the way in which we see the world. (2000:15)

Story-telling may be transformative. The evidence lies in the way stories themselves change, not simply by giving a happy ending to something whose meaning depended on the tragedy lying at its heart. As we suggested it is the kind of story which undergoes a metamorphosis rather than any particular events taking place within it. In the stories which heal us it is not so much the things which happen but the way they are presented. Sadness, trauma, hopelessness are the realities with which a person's or group's story must somehow deal, but there are other things – deliverances, hilarities, profound emotional satisfactions, moments of joy, personal and group achievements – which must also be registered, and registered in a way which allows them to have the narrative weight they deserve. When we use story as a vehicle for the way we actually experience life rather than the way we look backwards or forwards from some fixed point within it, a kind of theoretical 'now' which can never really be grasped except as a kind of jumping-off point for what we remember or expect – or hope for – then we use a different kind of story, one designed to express and embody continuity and involvement in the process of living. For this kind of experience, neither tragedy nor comedy is really enough. The subject to be explored here is our experience of life in flux, work in progress, so that too much concentration on those times when, through trauma or release, life actually stood still may, because of their drama, actually distort the message we are delivering. They will always be essential reference points in the narratives we put together, but ongoing life needs another kind of story-telling, too.

The narrative form which group work finds most useful for the ongoing business of exploring its own life together is neither comedy nor tragedy but romance – life seen as an ever-changing picture, a landscape we travel over in the hope of arrival at a final destination; although the imagery of voyaging through storm and fair weather, shipwreck and island-fall, bound for a succession of ports of call before finally reaching harbour, comes closer to the essence of the genre. Because of its expansiveness, romance provides the story-teller with room to manoeuvre. Its terrors are set within the reassurance of an outcome which, however delayed or postponed it may be, will eventually prove favourable. The actual personages of romance are obviously 'creatures of the imagination', but the way in which they come and go is inescapably realistic. Romance offers us a literary format we can use to express and embody whatever we wish:

> Romance peoples the world with fantastic, normally invisible
> personalities or powers ... its typically episodic theme is
> perhaps best described as the theme of the boundary of

consciousness. (Northrop Frye 1957:57)

Because of this it is able to express itself with exceptional directness simply because it can say things which other more realistic ways of describing life cannot find words for. Caliban, for example, is an obvious monster, something dreamed up by his master, Prospero. His *realism* is the truth of lawlessness and indiscipline and this shines out without any attempt to be 'lifelike': Caliban is what he is, and the play allows him to be it. He is not intended to be a person like ourselves, only to be unavoidably relevant to our situation if we choose to see it that way. Romance's advantage as a literary genre is its ability to contain things, to treat conclusions as stages, to transcend failures and hopelessness by continually extending its own framework; for romance is the adventurer's tale, the journey into identity which reminds us who we are in terms of who we might be. Because of this it remains lifelike, for whether we like it or not, the arrangements we make for living are always provisional ones. The extemporised nature of drama and story – and even the best rehearsed plays and familiar stories are in this sense extemporised, made up in order to run parallel with the life situation which we actually inhabit, so that one way or another we may learn from the experience. As the story develops its tone changes (this again is a characteristic of romance); different ideas are tried out, bringing with them new forms of expression. This can happen wherever people meet to tell stories about themselves; they repeat a joke, sing a song, show off a new article of clothing. Most strikingly of all it happens when they are actively encouraged to be inventive, given permission to explore what has happened to us and compare it with whatever is happening now, in the present. Thus so far as self-expression goes, the group provides place and time for story, just as the story does for the group.

(d)   Acting the Island

Art itself has been described as "an environment in which personal change can occur" (Aldridge 1996:245). Embodied art realises changes dramatically, its medium being the way we behave both alone or in company. Drama is the most immediate form of exploration of what it is like to be a person among persons. The following is a story enacted by a group of people wishing to explore the terms of their own inter-relationship. Because it is never easy to plunge straight into this kind of group action, in which people taking part get used to living in a world of shared imagination, I include it as a group who took part described it, omitting the group leader's instructions.

- We stood in a circle and told everyone our name.
- We imagined standing on a beach. We could hear the surf roaring in the distance. Then we closed our eyes and simply felt the sun on our face and smelled the breath of the sea. We moved our feet in the sand, feeling it beneath our soles and between our toes. We put down roots into the earth below and swayed like trees in the wind blowing from the sea.
- We held one another's hands and swayed all together first one way and then the other. We imagined we were the waves of the sea beating up against the cliffs and shores of the island.
- We opened our eyes and began to explore the place, moving around the room as if it were a real island, kicking our feet through the dry sand, walking on sun-baked patches and places where the sea had left ridges in it, then clambering over rocks, discovering pools, each of us finding our own things to do before exploring our way into the island itself.
- We found partners and walked round the island with them, showing each other what we found there, what we liked and didn't like, what we found interesting and why.
- We found crayons and paints in the 'cave' and drew or painted a map, working together as a couple.
- We put the maps together and compared them, asking and answering questions about them if we could.
- All together we arranged the space to become an ideal island, each person contributing a particular feature or aspect.
- Sitting on the ground, some of us in the sun and some in more sheltered positions, we listened to music and thought about what we had been doing.
- As a group we shared things which had occurred on the island. Were they anything like things which happened within the group? What did the physical features of the island represent?

Afterwards, one of those taking part made the following comment:

> The island maps seemed strangely like one another, because they all had more or less the same kind of shape. I was reminded of an amoeba (something very basic) or perhaps a foetus (something not yet properly developed). There

was a tendency to have a semi-circular northern shoreline, sometimes with cliffs or rocks, and a broad sandy bay scooped out of the southern part. I don't know why this should be the case, because the pairs of cartographers didn't seem to be conferring at all at this stage.

I remember noticing this myself and being fascinated by it. During the discussion at the end of the session someone suggested that the as yet unborn child might possibly represent the group itself which really hadn't developed into a proper group at this stage. Perhaps it was because we were all to some extent or other 'testing the waters'.

The session described above took place at the beginning of a group process which continued for some months, in which those involved went on finding out more about themselves, both as individuals and as group members as time went on. It turned out to have been a fruitful way of beginning to work together, although when I first thought of getting people to concentrate on the image of an island it was as a way of providing a framework for exercises in group co-operation – which indeed it turned out in the event to be.

In the event it was when we were really 'in it' that the power of the island symbolism asserted itself and we began to find out what 'being together' really meant. It was not simply a matter of learning new facts, practising unfamiliar skills, but of the level of learning and practising, the measure of our involvement in what was happening to us: our birth as a group. Certainly the notion of being shipwrecked together on an island provided us with a work-space for trying out new ideas of how to get along together; but a symbolic laboratory has its own ways of working.

Particularly when the symbolism is of oceans and islands. In this instance the powerful imagery of problems shared and individual differences worked through. Above all, it is of human inter-dependence and co-operation. Alastair Campbell, writing about pastoral counselling, criticises one-to-one approaches as failing to penetrate to the heart of the matter which is traceable to the dominance of impersonal social attitudes rather than personal pathologies:

> Christian pastoral counselling should surely be capable
> of bringing to society an awareness of finitude, of the
> uselessness of running away from the pain necessary for
> living, and of the oneness of all that God has created.
> (1979)

For pastoral care to be relevant to the situation in which we find ourselves, "we need to rediscover what Alan Watts called 'the wisdom of insecurity'. To do this, however, we must somehow be able to launch fearlessly into the unknown." Instead, however, we continue to treat one another as though our lives belong to us in some distinctly separable way, "as isolated individuals adrift in the world" (1979).

On our island, however, things were different. As someone said, "I really feel we were all in it together." This was largely because within the island situation the experience of discovery was essentially a shared project. Learning, in this laboratory, was both individual and corporate, and so was caring. In fact, the two were in harmony. Unfortunately some of our approaches to pastoral care have managed to divide learning from caring by a strict apportioning of roles according to which the knowers (who are, of course, also the carers) are set over against those who don't know, one of their main areas of ignorance being that of caring for themselves and other people. The experience of being a person among people is the main area of study for the kind of pastoral care envisaged by island symbolism. The extent to which our personal experience relates to our understanding of Christian belief lends itself to pastoral care of a specifically church-centred kind; but the island is there to be visited even without a guidebook which can tell us precisely what we are looking for and how we should set about searching for it. In a book which appeared several years ago I drew attention to the tendency of the church to prefer using didactic ways of dealing with scripture to alternative approaches.

> There are always people who seem to want to do the Bible's job for it. Instead of letting it speak for itself they want to tell you what it says and precisely how it applies to you. But what is valuable from the point of view of a group work approach is not so much the conclusions reached as the experience of simply sharing the journey. (2002:2)

When the conclusions are reached by means of an experience of imaginative sharing they are all the more likely to be taken personally and have a more notable effect on the way we see one another and our world.

CHAPTER 6
Exile

(a)   Severance

Welcome, sir.
This cell's my court; here have I few attendants
And subjects none abroad; pray you look in ...
(*The Tempest* Act V sc.1)

Prospero's words are full of irony, coming as they do at the very moment when his fortunes are so triumphantly reversed and his dukedom restored; but they are also deeply pathetic. By the time the gift stolen from him is restored he finds he has largely outgrown its satisfactions. What seems to be exile from everything which made his life worth living – except, of course, his baby daughter and the remnants of his cherished library – has turned out in a way he never expected (as indeed life tends to do). While Prospero has been on his island it is not only the busy world which has moved on. He has moved on too; and it has not been a totally negative experience by any means, giving him the opportunity he has craved to deal with unfinished business weighing heavily on his soul and providing him with the opportunity he needed to develop the particular skills necessary for the task:

I have bedimm'd
The noontide sun, call'd forth the mutinous winds
And twixt the green sea and the azur'd vault
Set roaring war ... (Act V sc.1)

These things and others like them were not performed for their own sake, but to bring about the state of affairs in which he will be able to set the record straight in the way he craves, by an action of extreme magnanimity in which the real man transcends the magician:

> You, brother mine, that entertain'd ambition
> Expell'd remorse and nature ... I do forgive thee.
> (Act V sc.1)

Not all exile is as propitious as this, however. The word itself implies a painful kind of separation without any suggestion of relief, of time well spent. It is more or less synonymous with separation and summons up ideas and perhaps memories of deprivation or even abandonment.

The experience of being forsaken has deep resonances for a Christian culture. Depth analysis and Christian theology have many fascinating correspondences, the most obvious of them being St Paul's understanding – an orthodox Old Testament one – of original sin, and Freud's teaching about the id, both referring to human conditions in which 'good' as opposed to 'bad' has no connection with 'right' as opposed to 'wrong'. In other words the primal selfishness in which there is only self to be considered. Both Christianity and psychoanalysis regard this state of affairs as one which requires and receives drastic modification through the action of an outside authority, either God or the truth involved in being human, "the real external world which surrounds us". According to both anthropologies, human nature is changed for the better by this intervention while still yearning, at another level of its being, for the worse:

> For I do not the good I want, but the evil I do not want is what I do. Now if I do that I do not want, it is no longer I that do it, but sin that dwells within me. (*Romans* 7:19-20)

or as Freud describes the situation:

> The oldest portion of the mental apparatus [the *id*] remains important through life. (1949:2*n*)

The experience described is a nostalgic longing for a condition of total satisfaction with things as they are – or *the thing as it is* – without the complication of having to choose among alternative ways of living and being perpetually tempted to choose the least thoughtful, preferring ones which offer the speediest release of the tension involved in having to choose at all. Things which are, according to the new condition of humanity, immature, unreflective and unaware of other's needs assume a seductive power to attract us away from what we are aware of as authentic characteristics of our condition as psychologically well-adjusted and/or redeemed women and men.

Both Paul and Freud regard the movement from 'before' to 'after' as providing much more than a change in the way we think about ourselves and the world. For psychoanalysis id-awareness is qualitatively different from the way in which the ego approaches the task of making sense of its environment. Indeed, from the ego's point of view the id has no environment, being always simply itself. Similarly the human universe before the Fall was severely restricted in scope; or rather it was a different kind of scope, possessing depth of belonging without ideational complexity – which is one of the reasons why world-weary men and women yearn for its simplicity, envisaging a time and place with none of the complications attaching to every time and place which real people experience – or have ever experienced. It is this blissful absence of effort, effort to make reasonable sense, which renders this pre-enlightened condition so very seductive. This is the simplicity we crave so much and mythologise as various forms of Eden. It is, however, a forbidden condition, one from which, left to ourselves, we are consistently excluded.

The social arrangements made by human groups clearly show our profound awareness of the dynamics of inclusion-exclusion; and this reflects the way we make sense of the world in general. Wherever there is a structuring of experience exclusion takes place as the first stage of the cognitive process. The making of sense requires the disruption of nonsense; so much is obvious. What is not so immediately apparent, however, is the extent to which we actually need to make sense. Studies of human perception representing very different psychological traditions arrive at the same conclusion: that consciousness organises the things we perceive before we ourselves can make any sense of what is happening to us. For gestalt psychology the brain itself discovers analogues for meaning and order in the world in accordance with its own interior organization; for personal construct psychology our total view of life revolves around our own system of relating ideas and experiences, which is entirely dependent on the sense we have already made of things, as "a person's processes are psychologically channelised by the ways in which he anticipates events" (Kelly 1991). Thus, according to both gestalt and personal construct, before we know anything at all our minds are already telling us what kind of thing we should expect. The phenomenological psychology of Maurice Merleau-Ponty goes even further by claiming that our fore-knowledge of the world we perceive takes advantage of the fact that the reality we perceive as outside ourselves is actually working in close co-operation with us: what, for us, is 'out there' exists as a function of our relationship with it as

> the horizon whose distance from me would be abolished –
> since that distance is not one of its properties – if I were not
> there to scan it with my gaze. (1962: Introduction)

"Because we are in the world," says Merleau-Ponty, "we are condemned to meaning", not because the world we know depends on our capacity to organise sensations, but because of the intimate relationship between reality and the way it comes across to us; not because the mind imposes it, either organically or in terms of our own individual cognitive system-building, but because we somehow lend ourselves to it and receive ourselves from it. In religious terms, because we are created to exist together.

No wonder then that an experience or event which destroys this 'non-thetic communion' comes across as such a deprivation. This is the felt reality of the severance symbolised as our exclusion from Paradise as the place where we know we belong because we were made for it, and because not having made ourselves – although we reassure ourselves by imagining that we did – we cannot reconstruct ourselves as another kind of creature in another creation, this time a more inclusive one. Condemned to meaning, we long for an Eden where meaning is no longer problematic. In this way the content of paradise is read back from this side of the experience of its loss (this side of the Fall?) and forced to take on a symbolic rather than a literal reality, in which the signified is an idealised and undifferentiated expression of the signifier; that is, the experience we already know and are able to recognise. Its new symbolic simplification draws to itself a state of being where there is total and complete harmony and everything fits. The symbolic frame answers our human need to make sense of what we encounter; to experience it, in fact. Frameless experience is quite literally mindless.

Thus the symbol of Eden or Paradise expresses the awareness of being irresistibly beckoned into meaning which is the ungraspable fulfilment of cognition, understood not as the absence of structure, which is inconceivable, but as the attainment of an eternal structure of belonging. As human beings we find it impossible to envisage the total absence of the structures of perception, so we see our bliss in terms of a release from the endless search for structures which really satisfy. As Robert Browning put it with the succinctness of the poetic symbol:

O that a man's reach should exceed his grasp,
Else what's a heaven for? (*Andrea dell Sarto*)

According to the Bible we long for it because we once knew it intimately and have since been exiled from it. Here again psychological theory marches alongside religious doctrine. In Jung's words,

> Our psyche is set up in accord with the structure of the universe, and what happens in the macrocosm likewise happens in the infinitesimal and most secret reaches of the psyche. (1963:335)

Thus the original fall from grace recounted for us in *Genesis* is dramatically reproduced in psychodynamic theory by the trauma of birth itself, the unparalleled interruption of actually being born. According to Lacan, the separation of the child from its mother's womb creates its own epistemological reality, namely the birth of the individual unconscious whose purpose is quite simply *not to know*, because the knowledge of what has happened, what has been lost, is too painful to be endured. The caesura in human personal experience is too total for any kind of rational assimilation within awareness. This is the origin of (and receptacle for) all unthinkable things which will happen to us in our future lives. Freud himself refers to *das Unbegriff*, but Lacan calls it *le coupure* – the cut. It represents the caesura introduced into our awareness by the shock of the original severance under whose token all psychic pain of an intolerable kind is open to dismissal unto unconsciousness (1979:43).

Humankind divorced from its own identity is a theme which runs through the world in one mythology or another. In Jungian terms it is the archetype of 'the Wanderer' whose presence lives on always within the knowledge which is shared at an unconscious level by the entire human race: mankind divorced from its true identity and searching for a lost awareness which forever escapes it. We are told in Genesis, itself a book about birth and beginning, that our urge to move beyond ourselves, to anticipate a way of making sense which is not freely open to us has had the effect of alienating us from what we will continue to construe as our real place in life, our authentic human heritage. As a race we remain conscious of this primal displacement whose effect is inter- as well as intra-psychic. What happened in the story happened to the species and its individual effect is transmitted to the individuals who comprise society. The drama is depicted as both universal and also final:

He drove out the man, and at the east of Eden he placed

the cherubim, and a sword flaming and burning to guard
the way to the tree of life. (*Genesis* 3:24)

So powerful is the image of deprivation that it occurs in mythologies
of a secular or even atheistic kind. For Marx it constitutes the basis of an
entire world-view according to which a large section of society, the largest
in fact, has suffered "social alienation" by being excluded from the fruits
of its own labours. Poggi descries the process as one in which

Relations that have resulted from a given historical process
may be treated, in the face of all evidence that their origins
are in the recent past, as timeless elements of nature itself.
(1972:103)

(b)   You're on your own

Thus the actual circumstances contributing to economic and social
exclusion are accorded a mythological resonance and immutability.

Emile Durkheim took a more hopeful view of shared mythologies,
looking forward to a time when society would be both able and willing
to proclaim its solidarity solely in terms of those values of mutual co-
operation and personal respect which were for him the authentic religious
categories of a developed civilisation, in which the increasing specialisation
of individuals' social function would inevitably lead to a higher level of
personal self-awareness and a more developed sense of social responsibility.
The language of this new corporate consciousness would fulfil the same
function as that carried out by the mythological codes of religion in the
socially and occupationally undifferentiated societies of former times. The
shared imagery of religious belief was, for him, the symbolic instrument
of the moral awareness which characterises social experience.

Collective thought transforms everything it touches. It fuses
natural orders and combines contraries; it reverses what one
might regard as the natural hierarchy of being, it eliminates
differences and differentiates between what is similar.
(1953:94)

Here then is a nineteenth century doctrine of the redemption of
humanity from its post-Edenic captivity, by the superior social consciousness
of a developed civilisation. It is supported by Durkheim's view of the
alternative state of affairs, the situation which exists for those who are

unable to take advantage of it. People who see the world as a reality they feel unable to engage with are suffering, he says, from a high degree of *'anomie'* – the precise opposite of social solidarity. The literal meaning of the word is 'namelessness'. People in this condition are aware of the world as impersonal, uncontrollable, shapeless and ceaselessly changing, because they cannot locate themselves in any of the arrangements it makes for living. They do not fit, and consequently have no name by which to be known and know themselves.

The effect of anomie on individuals is to make them feel that they are less than persons. However although its result is anti-personal, its origin lies in conditions outside personal control, as it signifies a state of affairs characterised by the extreme shortage of viable norms of social action, which Durkheim himself was acutely conscious of in his own generation. This was a problem which could only be solved by organised co-operative action. Individual effort will not suffice.

(Anomie) springs from the lack of collective forces at
certain points in society: that is, of groups established for
the regulation of social life. (1970:382)

Like the parallel concept of alienation, anomie is used to describe a condition which is both social and individual, but is basically a product of a view of society as having some sort of power of its own which depends entirely on the willingness and ability of individual persons to surrender their individuality to it and conform to its rules.

Again we may be reminded of 'man's first disobedience' as the similarity between sociological and religious ways of looking at life becomes clearer. Both sociology and politics have their share of texts regarded by devotees as holy writ; and because the kind of thinking and arguing which characterises this form of circular presentation requires both to draw conclusions of pan-humankind from the actual histories of individuals and groups of people. In other words, both assume the authority of myth.

(c)   Wanderers

Psychologically, politically, sociologically, the same picture emerges: that of a race excluded from bliss by its own efforts to deny the truth about itself in basic matters concerning human vulnerability and need for mutuality. This is the 'genesis paradigm' as it continues to be relived at an anthropological level in varying forms of cultural expression throughout the world from religious narratives and folklore to novels, plays and comic books. C.G. Jung's 'theory of archetypes' is a great source of illumination for those who wish to explore this kind of imagery. The archetype represents an "inborn mode of psychic apprehension" associated with personages drawn from the shared unconscious of the human race throughout the world. The scenarios of exclusion and exile which we have been considering in connection with our island image suggest two of these recurrent themes: one – the Wanderer – typifying the action of searching for rest and completion; the other expressing the safety and wholeness we imagine having experienced in the maternal womb – the Mother.

> Like any other archetype, the mother archetype appears
> under an almost infinite variety of aspects. The archetype is
> often associated with things and places standing for fertility
> and fruitfulness. (1972:15)

In this connection Jung draws specific attention to gardens. This, however, is the garden-paradise from which the Wanderer is shut out and for which he searches. The process is arduous, even hazardous, but the search brings its rewards in terms of the growth of character and the scope it gives for genuinely personal relationships. Describing the Wanderer archetype Carol Pearson writes that:

> Whether Wanderers journey only inward or also outward
> they make a leap of faith to discard the old roles which they
> have worn to please and ensure safety, and try instead to
> discover who they are and what they want. During their
> travels they find a treasure that symbolically represents the
> gift of their true selves. (1944:51)

Thus, according to analytical psychology, the exile's journey away from what was once home is psychoformative, as the problems of an often hostile environment, both of people and circumstances are encountered and overcome. It is a journey away, but also a journey back. In line with religious symbols, the imagery points both ways. What lies behind is always ahead; it is only direct access which is henceforth forbidden. Setting out in the opposite direction the Wanderer is refreshed from time to time with the vision of what awaits her or him at journey's end. It is these fore-tastes of homecoming which make the journey bearable, for

> Many a green isle needs must be
>
> In the deep wide sea of misery

Or the mariner, worn and wan
Never thus could voyage on. (P.B. Shelley, *Lines Written
among the Euganean Hills*, 1818)

Prospero found such an isle. Or rather, he found a deserted island and peopled it for his own immensely serious kind of entertainment. Thus "going through the valley of misery" he "used it for a well" (Ps. 84:6). The relevance of this for pastoral theology is that very many people regard religion itself in such a way, as a spiritual task undertaken for the healing of a psychological wound. Because of its total and permanent nature this wound cannot be dealt with psychologically. It needs another kind of remedy altogether, one which "passes understanding". This approach is in and from another direction, and requires acceptance of the wound, not any attempt to control its effect by technical expertise or psychological explanation: faith alone is the answer. Thus Christians pray "that among the many changes of this world, our hearts may surely there be fixed where true joys are to be found" (Common Worship, Collect for 3rd Sunday before Lent) and the Qur'an tells of "A Garden the breadth whereof is as the breadth of heaven and earth" (ch.57).

Religious solutions are transcendent by definition. All the same a psychological wound, even one of such overriding human significance as experiencing ourselves severed from the source of joy, the means of life, calls for understanding of a kind which takes its impact into account. Pastoral care should have the therapeutic insight to do this without relying upon the religious faith of people who have psychological problems. As we have seen, human beings are a profoundly traumatised species; the evidence is both public and private, in corporate decisions and individual life histories. To conclude that our religious awareness has a profound effect on our psychological state and vice versa is not to limit religion in any way, but simply to draw attention to the reciprocity of our relationship with transcendence. Our experience is responsive and we are not always in a position to respond optimally by making the very best of what is being offered.

Many mental health professionals regard religion and religious ways of explaining human experience as totally unacceptable because of its unwillingness to approach problems from the point of view of scientific method. Some views of human psychological process have chosen to regard things which can be measured as the only valid source of knowledge about how human beings function – and indeed what kind of entity human beings actually are. The discovery of hidden sources of behaviour and experience did not stop psychoanalysis, for instance, from including them within the realms of science; they were simply unknowable science, science taken on trust through the belief one has about its omnipotence. Meanwhile behavioural psychology ignores intangibles as irrelevant, the unnecessary sequlae of previous behaviour which alone gives rise to the things we do and feel, and the explanation we give ourselves for doing and feeling them

(d)   Hoping for Heaven

This chapter's argument is unlikely to commend itself to those who argue along these lines, based as it is on the proposition that people's lives are drastically affected by a trauma of deprivation which applies at both the racial and the individual level, yet cannot be assimilated in the way we have been trained to set about tackling the problems which we encounter in life because the original trauma pre-empts argument. Perhaps Frank Lake in Clinical Theology (1966) comes closest to holding psychology and religion together, although he does so in a way which seems closer to medicine than it does to spirituality.

For the notion of original sin Lake substituted the idea of original suffering on the part of individual men and women. Led by his knowledge of psychiatry and by psychological insights of his own he went considerably further than earlier pastoral theologians had done to forefront the healing effect upon individuals of the forgiveness of their sins. The forgiveness brought about by Christ's death and resurrection is deeply personal and totally efficient in its ability to transform those whom it touches by neutralising not only human sinfulness, but every other kind of evil affecting men and women:

> He reconciles to God by His cross not only sinners but
> sufferers. (1980)

The homologisation of two kinds of breakdown, spiritual and physical certainty simplifies the task of pastoral theology, making its area of concern the healing of a spiritual or relational 'lesion' corresponding to the malfunctions which occur in clinical medicine. From one point of view this is a clear recognition of the role of the spiritual, explicitly promoted here as the specific, unique treatment for a particular category of evil affecting human beings. The forgiveness of Christ frees mankind from the condemnation attaching not only to deliberately chosen sin, but also the ways in which mind and body have interacted to produce various forms of mental illness. In this way Lake's approach applies to those who do not confess their sins as well as those who do. Suffering which cannot be aligned with any discoverable offence is explained in terms of unacknowledged pain which lies outside the reach of our conscious need for repentance. The source of hidden distress refers to events believed to have taken place during the first few months and years of life, or even before we were actually born in the first place. This version of the primal severance scenario has been backed up by evidence of an unorthodox kind. The use of LSD within a pastoral context resulted in testimonies of spiritual experience taking place in utero, harmonised by Lake and his associates with biblical texts in the effort to demonstrate how far back in her or his awareness an individual's separation anxiety actually reaches, and the extent of its ability to bear witness to the truth revealed in holy scripture.

This is very different from Viktor Frankl's (1973) existential analytical approach which claims that psychological healing depends on the action of detaching ourselves spiritually from whatever it may be that is actually happening, and by placing ourselves in God's hands, carry out a leap of faith into the freedom to which he is summoning us. For Lake, it is not merely belief in God which heals and restores us, but a very precise and definite response to pain which must be contacted by the therapist and used for healing. A major task of psychotherapy, according to Lake, is to relieve the results of primal human trauma. The use of hallucinogenic drugs provides a means of exploring areas of the mind out of reach of verbal forms of psychiatric intervention; right-hemispherical thought (thinking which does not depend on words) is used to contact experiences too powerful and undifferentiated for ordinary expression and investigation permits access to the primary process thinking believed to characterise the way in which the unborn register what is happening to them.

This combination of neuro psychiatry and biblical hermeneutics is intentional. Indeed it is the whole point of Clinical Theology which is an extended and intensely systematic attempt to tie down Christian healing and thereby avoid Frankl's refusal to be explicitly religious in a doctrinal sense. It is a precise and definite response to Christ which heals, rather than a vague, unspecific belief in God; and what happens is the straightforward transference of an individual's suffering to a person who is willing to take it on board.

The sight of him, in the same extremity, enables us to move

from the spectacle of the one to the sight of the other,
annealing the images, until the Holy Spirit has effected a
transformation, a reconciliation, a peace and the beginning
of praise. (1980:2)

Lake's view of mankind is straightforwardly based on

The recorded aspects of the human and Godward
relationships of Christ. (1986:11)

To those who requested that he should revise his model, "eliminating
the biblical and faith dimension", he replied that

They are not scientific but emotional reasons which give rise
to the mood which dismisses faith statements of one order
(the religious) out of hand while swallowing whole scientific
assumptions which are faith statements of another order.
(1986:13)

Others have criticised Clinical Theology from the other direction,
maintaining that it claims to be too scientific rather than not scientific
enough. Robert Lambourne in particular was suspicious of what he and
others regarded as an alliance between two kinds of fundamentalism,
claiming that Lake used descriptions of mental states rather like Freud
himself did; that is, identical with the states themselves rather than products
of the creative imagination pointing in the direction of an ungraspable
reality. Human experience may be manipulated, certainly, but its essence
and wholeness escape our attempts to trace them in any way that we can
use as a total substitute for them. The Bible may tell us, even sometimes
shows us, divinity without being identical with God; in the same way
someone diagnosed as suffering from schizophrenia is not just a diagnosis.
Lambourne criticises Clinical Theology by claiming that

Insights from introspection were claimed to give
technological tools which could extract psychic defects.
(1966:17)

He maintains, on the contrary, that such insights, given extensive
diagrammatic (he would say 'pseudo-diagrammatic') form in Lake's
writings are actually creative in themselves, without being translated 'line
for word' into the language of theo-psychopathology.

Lake, like psychopathological theorists in general, was concerned with
hermeneutics, the effort to make sense of something in terms of something
else, one world-view in terms of another. Lambourne is not suggesting that

the two weltanschauungen, psychopathology and religion, have nothing in common, simply that they are not congruent and ought not to be synthesised, because both are essentially symbolic ways of knowing as opposed to literal ones. Both contain literal elements within a poetic framework, the irreducible poetry of persons and of God. One thing binds a psychological or psychotherapeutic and a theological one together, and that is the mythology, universal and individual, of severance, whether this is seen in terms of Lacan's dramatic 'cut' or Milton's epic poem, for both in fact tell the same story, that

Of man's first disobedience, and the fruit
Of that forbidden tree. (*Paradise Lost*, Book I line 1)

For pastoral care the story remains one which should never be forgotten or overlooked, because it concerns all involved – carers and cared-for alike. It lies behind all our unbidden emotions and adds its unspoken weight to the things we consider rational. It accounts for the times when we over-react – or think we do – and the times when other people's reactions appear to us to be out of scale with what is actually happening to them or to ourselves. It is the hidden wound, the unfinished business, the suggestion of which we find so disconcerting. At another level of immediacy, it is the play we see or the book we read which has so disturbingly emotional an effect – which seems so very personal, even though we can't actually remember anything even remotely like that ever happening to us. In everyday life it is the dependably cheerful friend or colleague who suddenly breaks down in tears, or the fit of anger from the person whose self-control has always impressed us so much.

We are not talking about character here, but about something deeper than that; something which the best efforts of ourselves and other people have not managed to get rid of, a weakness within human nature itself which lets us down when we are not expecting it to do so, sometimes in the very times and places where we are accustomed to feel most confident of our ability to cope with life, when we are congratulating ourselves at having managed to overcome. I suppose this is what is actually being described as usually attributed to 'just being human', which is actually what it is, of course. Or rather, it is 'being human' without the 'just'. Because it is so ordinary, it is therefore not unimportant, although we are accustomed to distracting ourselves from its effects by attributing them elsewhere, to psychic traumas which we can – either by ourselves or with some professional help – locate among the events of our lives and home in on as the origins of our personal distress.

This is not to say that such life crises have not played their part in any distress we are feeling now, or that this should not be acknowledged. Denying such things certainly makes the situation worse, reinforcing as it is bound to do our established habit of denial, according to which we are used to saying to ourselves first and then to other people, that we are perfectly all right and don't need any help. But it is not these things but the background against which they have always taken place which should be acknowledged in our attempts to understand and to help. Perhaps we can only help ourselves by trying to help others; but we can only help anybody, other people or ourselves, by accepting the fact of woundedness, both ours and theirs.

Pastoral care must therefore look further than argument about what it may or may not be that has brought about someone's immediate distress even when this draws so much of its force from things in the past now remembered or half-remembered – or remembered with assistance. The origin of the pain lies earlier, in a condition which impacts upon the entire race, a separation from the possibility of a condition of happiness that belongs specifically to human beings caused by the abrogation of the circumstances which allowed that condition to go on existing. Thrust into the world, nothing we ourselves bring can heal such a wound apart from our chronic need to feel ourselves restored. Only love can set our world right: generalised acceptance, an atmosphere of kindness, techniques of caring, somewhere to be while we draw on our own recuperative powers, none of these things turns out to be deep or lasting enough. A severed self needs more than this.

Psychodynamic investigation into the emergence of human personality reveals that our own attempts to renew ourselves have not been as successful as we would like to think they have been. Indeed many of the problems we have with other people – and they with us – originate in the failures we have had in coping with life in the way we think we ought to have done. Perhaps we have been fortunate and found someone, or a succession of people, whose love for us has "passed understanding" (their understanding of us, that is!). What is certainly true is that any healing we have received has come from someone else's involvement in our concerns. Somebody has cared enough for us to put up with us, in fact. Somebody else, not ourselves; because it is only when we care for somebody else enough to put ourselves into their hands that we are genuinely aware of having a self at all.

Self, it appears, is what we exchange with others and it is this interchange which gives life to all our relating.

Lovers know this, of course, and so do genuinely religious people. For religion the source of true healing is a transcendent Other. As the Baha'i prayer puts it:

Nearness to Thee is my hope, and love for Thee is my companion.
Thy mercy to me is healing.

while a Sikh exhorts believers to

Look where you may
He pervades and prevails
As love and affection.

Certainly we more readily associate interpersonal love with religion than with psychotherapy. And yet the therapist's regard for her or his client has many of the qualities of a loving relationship while managing to steer clear of some of the pitfalls which distort what passes for the purest and most selfless love in other settings. Love is not to be gauged according to the strength or weakness of the psychological ties which bind people together. Psychological bonding is certainly indispensable for preserving alliances necessary for the survival of individuals and continued existence of social groups, but this kind of belonging together is by no mean a guarantee of love or even of mutual understanding and acceptance. In the same way we may be emotionally close to someone, love them and be sure they return our love, but there are things we avoid saying to them in case they feel threatened or hurt, things we would rather just keep to ourselves; and we may be sure that the same also goes for them, although we would rather not dwell on the fact. The closer we get to these people who play such a vital part in our lives, the more important it becomes to preserve the status quo so that no-one gets upset. These are not big things, major admissions or fundamental complaints; in fact they may seem to us absurdly trivial, hardly worth mentioning to someone who knows us as well as this person does. In fact they know us too well, and we know what their response is likely to be. We know that whatever we say will not actually surprise them very much, they know us so well. What we want is a clean slate – or at least an unbiased ear.

(e)   Learning to Listen

This is precisely what therapeutic counselling aims to provide. The agreement to listen and not to judge is fundamental to the contract. The actual details of the agreement are not so important as the fact of having one. Contracts allow mutuality without intimacy; or rather, the intimacy they allow makes as few demands on a client's privacy as possible. It is not an invasive intimacy. Counsellors work hard to avoid the blackmailing approach which families appear to specialise in; they try not to say things like "You've got to tell me because …". They and their clients treat each other as caring strangers; caring enough to listen and to try and understand, strangers enough to respect each other's privacy.

Above all, caring enough to listen. Any kind of psychological healing depends on our willingness to put ourselves into the hands of others. We do this every time we really listen to someone else, concentrating on what they mean and not allowing ourselves to be distracted by some inner voice of our own. Then we have real contact with them and they with us; when we relinquish our characteristic defensiveness and speak out as we really feel. At such times our individuality is refreshed by 'dialogic imagination' (the phrase is Michael Bakhtin's), the fundamental action of giving and receiving in which we receive ourselves again and again from the hands of someone else – someone who really pays attention to us.

- I told her [the counsellor] what I really felt. She said she wanted to hear. She really listened to me. No-one else has listened like that. I told her all sorts of things.
- I realised that he [the counsellor] always waited before actually answering. Other people want to sort you out straight away, before you've really got round to telling them anything at all.
- I find that if I really level with them [the clients] they really listen. They can tell straight away if I'm just 'being a counsellor'.
- If they [the clients] ask me to say what I think about something it is vital to tell them; otherwise the relationship becomes false. It's because of the relationship that you can tell them, isn't it?

This ability to trust their clients is something which has not come at all easily to psychotherapy. The scientific study of behaviour and the mechanisms concerned with producing it lent itself to doctrines of objectivity and scientific rigour which made it difficult for practitioners to allow themselves to share freely and willingly in the process of exploration, which in fact they were involved in as participants and not simply as observers. If the aim was to render psychotherapy impersonal and dispassionate they failed because the professional boundaries against invasiveness on their own or their clients' part resulted in the creation of the kind of structured yet personal relationship in which clients feel safe enough to share. The rules of non-invasiveness and confidentiality which govern the therapeutic relationship provide vulnerable people with an unique opportunity to 'be themselves' – to bring their woundedness and rejection into a space where they can feel safe enough to let these things be seen.

The aim is not any kind of takeover, but the relationship which depends on separation; what Robert Hobson calls "aloneness togetherness" (1985). Client and counsellor are connected but not fused together. The mutuality is asymmetrical as the counsellor-therapist encourages her or his client in the discovery of a deeper sense of self to rediscover themselves. Such things take time to develop. It is not a case of inculcating new ways of behaving or providing any particular script to be followed; what is learned is a special way of communicating which grows up between two people together in their aloneness. In fact the urge to direct and control is the enemy of the therapeutic relationship. There must be space 'between' in which the awareness of communication, of being neither ignored nor crowded out can develop, and the self re-emerge as itself once again. In this relationship of self and other, the togetherness subsists in both concentrating on the same difficulty, and the aloneness in neither person making demands on the other.

The result can be, and very often is, a special relationship of trust which is unambiguous and gratuitous in the sense of being given without the emotional ties which characterise other relationships. It is only possible because it is to a certain extent mutual. The counselling relationship draws this kind of involvement from the therapist whose job it is to teach it to the client so that they can enjoy it together. In Paul Halmos's words:

> The counsellors have been shown to profess, openly or by implication that they consider their warm personal attachment to the help-seeker as a vital instrument of helping. (1965:74)

The clients themselves certainly respond:

- For once I could say what I felt without hurting anyone; for once being honest didn't run the risk of not being loved.
- I had permission to admit things which I wouldn't have said in anyone else's presence, because I knew she wouldn't go off me. She just wanted to know how I felt and what I thought.
- I felt it was OK just being me.

This is a relationship of unconditional mutual regard which might be taken as a paradigm for pastoral caring because of its ability to go back to another relationship characterised by acceptance, the permission to be ourselves which we long for and which lies always out of reach. It would be misleading to suggest that this kind of relationship between therapist and client always exists; but if a therapist aims at being a healer in fact as well as name, this is what he or she will have in mind at some level of awareness – the creation of an island-state of restoration and renewal which will have an effect of déjà vu for the client and for themselves and to which they will find themselves returning from time to time in the middle of their ordinary business.

It is the kind of involvement which encourages the wounded person to detach themselves from the effort they customarily make to cope with their pain by refusing to acknowledge its presence and being constantly reminded of it. Sharing of this kind, designed to take account of the reality of pain without being swamped by it, resembles Kenneth Pargament's description of the effect created by meditation, where pain is acknowledged in a special way:

> Rather than lose him or herself in the experience, the individual is asked to attend to the experience from a more distanced detached vantage point. (2007:257)

Here, then, is one of the most healing things about a relationship which allows space for disclosure, in which we can be both distanced *from* and present *to* whatever is happening to us. From Prospero's mountain, we can take in the whole island. What we most need is someone to give us a leg up.

CHAPTER 7
Refuge

(a)   Vulnerability

> When the infant emerges into the world from the mother's
> womb a loud wail marks the entry of air into the lungs and
> the shock of exposure to the world. Without being asked
> the child is committed to the world and the life that lies
> ahead. If reluctant, the obstetrician holds the infant by
> the heels and raps them sharply, for this is the moment of
> decision. (Lidz 1983:3)

People are nervous about and of one another. The corollary to this,
of course, is that the more vulnerable we ourselves are, the more vividly
we tend to experience others as less vulnerable than ourselves. Theatre
is intended to be a place where nervousness of this kind – what we are
accustomed to call social or interpersonal anxiety – can be put on hold.
Theatre uses 'the suspension of disbelief' in order to achieve 'the suspension
of nervousness'. Certainly it doesn't happen automatically. Somebody has
to find the courage to go on stage themselves, in one way or another
to establish the fact that in this place, at this time, under these rules of
'let's pretend' true things about being human may be safely shared and
courageously explored. "Keep me as the apple of an eye, hide me under
the shadow of your wings" (Ps. 17:8). This ability to protect and expose
at the same time belongs also to liturgy, whose entire subject matter is
concerned with the most challenging and therefore potentially the most

terrifying of personal encounters, that between people and God. Looked at like this, from a theological point of view vulnerability and human-ness belong together. Vulnerability may take refuge in aggressiveness but this is unlikely to run very deep. However expressed or embodied the urge to remain secure is intrinsic to being human.

From this point of view my experience of being myself as vulnerable, drama and liturgy march together, including me within their scenarios of meeting and sharing which somehow manage to make me so much less scared than I would otherwise be, once I have managed to surrender some of my own defensiveness, the false confidence I have so painstakingly built up in my own ability to avoid self-exposure (except, of course, on my own terms). The stories which draw us out of ourselves in church and theatre involve us in an action of shared imagination which goes back to our very earliest awareness of other people as authentically other – like ourselves but definitely not ourselves.

As Freud made clear this is the most authentically human event in our lives. He called it "secondary identification", the awareness of other people which marks our entry into the world of real people ourselves. Freud was eager to point out the disruptive effect of such a discovery from a sexual point of view, but the anxiety of being forced to abandon our primary autonomy must precede even this in the history of personal awareness. If existence belongs to me, how can you have it too? In other words, if you are in fact you, then who is it I am? Our fear of other people demonstrates that the shock of not being completely autonomous has never completely worn off. That there should actually be other people strikes at the heart of my being myself, so that I can only adjust to it by developing control over their ability to be personal, filtering their reality out to prevent it from intruding on my own. The fear of being engulfed lurks in the background of the social life of individuals.

One of the purposes of pastoral care is to allow individual women, men and children to overcome their anxieties about making personal contact with one another and with the human world of which they are part. Holding back from contact is just too easy for us, not only because of the psychological defensiveness I have been talking about – which I believe affects everyone – but because this fear can be greatly increased by the various incidents which make up our own individual biographies. Babies are neglected and abused, schoolchildren bullied, workers subjected to systematic depersonalisation; inside the family itself relationships deteriorate and fall apart so that long-forgotten wounds are reopened.

Various civil tragedies occur and oppressive social tendencies worsen. All these things increase the human need for places of refuge, using the word 'place' both literally and metaphorically. If we use it literally we think of enclosures – wombs, walled gardens, every sort of sanctuary ranging from cupped hands to fortified castles. If we use it as a metaphor or a poetic way of talking about life and death it can be even more expressive, as the name given to the central reservation in busy streets which manages to sum up a universe of human vulnerability far beyond its actual meaning: 'the central refuge'. Actually this is usually described as a 'traffic island'; but the two ideas are very closely associated in most people's imagination, as for ship-wrecked mariners and pedestrians escaping from rush hour traffic the central reservation is certainly both an island and also a refuge.

Pastoral care involves the provision of such refuges, whether or not they are willing to be described as such. The image is a good one because it involves a degree of urgency, as we hurry to avoid being knocked down and run over by the approaching traffic. Refuges are places and times when urgency is over, or at least when it is blessedly interrupted. It is the opposite pole to urgency, the new reality, and as such it needs time to establish itself, as we do to inhabit it, although its reality was obvious enough at a distance. For people who have discovered a place to shelter from the storms of life, time may move more slowly, as life's actions and reactions lose their urgency. This, they say, is not merely the result of shock, the inevitable result of changes which are drastic. This is more like having plunged deep into the lagoon of quietness:

> I came desolate and bereft
> I found safety and peace
> A place where I could be me
> Where there is no judgement or condemnation. (2007:19)

Elizabeth Baxter quotes words written by a temporary visitor to Holy Rood House, a Centre for Health and Pastoral Care in the north of England. Contributing to a book inspired by Holy Rood, Baxter proposes what she calls a 'threshold theology'. This was only a short visit but for the person concerned it was an extremely urgent one. This is how Baxter describes the effect made on emotionally wounded people by their arrival at Holy Rood:

> I see the porch of Holy Rood House acting as a metaphor
> not only for the work of the community but also for the
> work and movement of the divine. Here is transitional
> space where vulnerabilities meet and embrace. Here hope
> is realised and the interface of safety and risk takes place.
> (2007:16)

It is only when we compare this with the settings provided for more scientific approaches to healing that we get anything like a true picture of Holy Rood House. Here an attempt has been made to create an atmosphere in which wounded people will feel genuinely at home. In some ways they may feel even more at home than they have ever been because a great deal of effort and a high degree of skill have been devoted to trying to find out what it is that makes a space healing; the mixture of ordinariness and difference, unexpected pleasure and reassuring routine, for instance. Much goes on at Holy Rood House which is comfortingly recognisable, a blessed contrast to the emotional trauma recently suffered. What comes as a surprise is the degree of receptiveness to personal need which characterises the organization as a whole.

(b) Refuge and Psychotherapy

All the same the presence of others is potentially a threat. Even a place like this, geared to the healing of wounds and the laying to rest of fears, contains other people; and as we said earlier, the more vulnerable a person is, the more nervous they are likely to be about others. There are, after all, other guests at Holy Rood House who might very well be less kind than the people running the place; and in any case, how do I know how kind they really are? This, of course, is what Elizabeth Baxter means by "transitional space where vulnerabilities meet and embrace". The drama of human interaction goes back a very long way, not only between people but within them too. Theatre demonstrates it most vividly as audiences and actors find themselves drawn two ways, into the play through the pity they feel for the people portrayed in it, and out of it in order to protect themselves from being to closely associated with what is going on there – the process Aristotle called catharsis, which is pity and fear when they are experienced at the same time and have a purgative effect on an audience's normally well-controlled feelings, allowing them to flow freely in the safety of the theatre.

This ancient technique works in theatres because it does in life, as Donald Winnicott demonstrated so vividly. Both psychotherapy and theatre work as enablers of personal encounter. They take place between and among persons, influencing the way in which they experience life. Both are concerned with the nature and quality of relatedness, and make use of space and time to do so. Certainly the importance of the setting in which an encounter takes place has always been recognised by drama, but not always by psychological forms of therapy, which have often aimed at being as impersonal – i.e. 'scientific' – as possible. Working with children, Winnicott's approach was strikingly different:

> ... she sat back on the couch with the Piggle beside her. Already I had made friends with the teddy bear who was sitting on the floor by the desk. Now I was in the back part of the room sitting on the floor playing with the toys. I said to the Piggle (whom I could not actually see): "Bring Teddy over here, I want to show him the toys." She went immediately and brought teddy over and helped me show him the toys. (1980:9)

Winnicott describes the action of taking leave of his desk in order to use part of his consulting room to fit the particular needs of one of his clients who is frightened by life 'in the real world'. Whatever happened between them would happen here, in dedicated space, before being translated into situations in the world outside. Indeed the idea of two ways of experiencing an adult person, one less frightened than the other, could only really be got across by changing the world in which this different kind of adult lived and moved. This was not simply another part of the room but another quality of room-ness, an imaginary place in which imaginary things happened. Sitting on the floor in the back part of the room and playing with toys, Winnicott had become a non-frightening person.

The experience of using space and time in this way sheds light on the union-in-separation which is relationship itself. This is not something which we all know about simply because we are human beings; or if we do, it is something we can very easily forget if life is too painful for us to allow us to take the chances involved in remembering and yet still persisting. It was, Winnicott points out, in the discovery of how to be safe-yet-daring that we discovered relationship to begin with. The distance between a child and its mother, "the separation that is not a separation but a form of union" (1971:115), is vulnerable, easily invaded and destroyed. Much distress and actual psychological pathology was the result of not having been able to enjoy and explore this betweenness. Because of parenting which was either neglectful or over-invasive or vacillated between the two extremes, the grieving child was psychologically wounded at an early stage of her or his development by being deprived of the space needed to form real relationships with others.

(b)   The Living Landscape

Space then is not empty. It is 'a landscape with figures'. The figures in it provide both succour and challenge. Refuge involves relationship and relationship is and must always be a balance between inclusion and alienation, a barrier overcome. Winnicott's theory, well-founded in practice, regards space and time as affecting individual's laboratories for exploring distance, opportunities for experimenting with ways of listing what is actually involved in being a person among people. This is what Winnicott calls "potential space" (1971:106-110). As in theatre, so in life: we meet its inhabitants within the sphere of embodied imagination, so that both spheres, concrete reality and fantasy, are experienced as equally true, equally real, "an intermediate area of experience that is not challenged"; and meeting them in such a special space we allow ourselves to share what is between us, owever painful. Relief from the immediacy of our own need for shelter sometimes opens us up to the presence of suffering which is not – or was not – our own. Distancing us from the world exposes us to one another, not simply to their threatening presence but also to our imaginative involvement. The exchange of empathy has a powerful effect on our personal worlds.

- It was the others who got me through. Someone put me in touch with somebody in the same position, someone who'd just arrived and didn't know anybody. We made a small group and that got me through. (Refugee: personal communication)
- I've always been a solitary kind of person. I like to do things by myself. Coach outings? I can't think of anything worse, and I've always been like this. But I'm all right here, because we're all a bit like that here. And some are worse than me. I try to get them talking. I think it helps them. (Depression support group member)

- When my brother came to this school – he's a year younger than me – he found me standing by myself, just here in the corner of the yard. I used to stand here by myself all break. Next time he brought a friend, and now we've got quite a group.
- The patients seemed to help one another more than the psychiatrists helped them. This is what they said, at least. The seating probably helped in a strange sort of way. It was arranged round the walls so you didn't have to look straight at anyone else, and certainly not at the people on each side of you. When people first arrived they sat staring in front of them, eyes fixed in the middle distance. When the time came for a patient to leave or someone was transferred to another part of the hospital, chairs had been moved out of place to make small social groups, so you could bet your life some kind of farewell party would be taking place in some part of the ward or other. (Hospital chaplain)
- I have noticed that self-help 'user groups' seem to generate a tremendous group loyalty. This may not involve the whole group, and probably won't, but it does refer to what you could call the group consensus on matters concerning the effect of social stigma and the management of mental illness. The opinion of the group is almost always considered to possess more authority than that of the CPN or even the psychiatrist. I don't think this can be written off as the effect of mental illness, as each user's diagnosis is probably slightly different; more likely it reflects the solidarity which comes from shared experience of a state of affairs which professionals only see 'from the outside'. (Community Psychiatric Nurse)

If safety is the refuge seeker's primary requirement, solidarity comes second. To be shipwrecked on a barren reef may quieten one's primary fears about survival, but if the reef is truly barren and you are the only person in it even the relief of still being alive may not last very long. This of course is the cruelty of solitary confinement. We may not always like one another, but we certainly always need one another. We may be in a splendid position to stand on our rock and proclaim like William James's crab that "I am myself, myself alone" (1902:8), but the very truth of what we say brings home to us the futility of saying it. Whatever we may actually be is only revealed to us in the experience of interchange. Actors learn their parts by imagining that they are saying their lines to an unseen 'other person' and imagination certainly does a great deal to help us feel real in the absence of any corroborating human presence. But as Bakhtin pointed out, it is in the essentially chancy business of putting ourselves at someone else's mercy merely by addressing them (for we need either their assent or their dissent as evidence that we ourselves exist) that our own sense of personhood subsists; and this is impossible to do if the other person is not actually there to receive me and respond to my gift with their own. I need them in order to be myself, and being myself is a two-way traffic.

For it to be a true refuge, there needs to be other people, at least another person, on this rock. In practical terms, of course, this has always been the case:

> the umbilical cord is cut and tied. The neonate or newborn
> appears puny and is helpless – among the most helpless of
> all creatures born into this world – and will require total
> care for a long time (Lidz 1983:3)

and emotional care for even longer; a whole lifetime, in fact. Sometimes the need for understanding and support becomes critical as the requirement for 'good enough' mothering is transformed during the first months and years into good enough *parenting*. Every step in the child's developing personality may be seen in terms of the underlying struggle which is taking place between conforming to other people's rule-making and expressive thoughts and feelings which even at this early age are recognisable as one's own and no-one else's. It is this central self which reaches out for acceptance, which, in the presence of rejection, seeks for refuge.

This infantile self-assertion grows and changes through interaction with others, producing the range of compromises which we call individual personality. The need to achieve a compromise between our own self-expression and other people's is more extreme, and consequently more painful at some periods in our lives than others. Developmental psychology recognises crises of self-identification, times in our lives when our relationship with others becomes strained, sometimes to breaking point, and particular relationships assume special intensity. The awakening of sexual awareness and its official ratification at puberty are two such crises, another occurring at mid-life.

In their intensity, developmental crises draw attention to the underlying need for security which characterises all human awareness. By itself, life is not enough for us; we need our lives established and ratified by another's voice raised or whispered in answer to our own. We need security of response, the meaning which human lives make in and among themselves. If it is not immediately forthcoming we will strive to get it, so that somehow we can re-discover ourselves. It does not necessarily have to be a human voice which answers us, so long as what it says remains intelligible.

(c)   Trust in God

In many instances the urge for 'security of response' assumes a form which is explicitly religious. As William James says:

> There is a state of mind known to religious men but to no others, in which the will to assist ourselves and hold our own has been displaced by a willingness to close our mouths and be as nothing in the floods and waterspouts of God. In this state of mind, what is most dreaded has become the habitation of our safety ... The time for tension in our soul is over and that of happy relaxation, of calm deep breathing, of an eternal presence with no discordant future to be anxious about, has arrived. Fear is not held in abeyance, as it is by mere morality, it is possibly expunged and washed away. (1902:47)

"To be as nothing in the floods and waterspouts of God": these are very religious people. Indeed most who regard themselves as religious would admit to being somewhat less confident of divine support than this. Many people's trust in God as ultimate deliverer comes second to their investment in more tangible security, like that promised by insurance companies; or, if there is a transcendent element in it this is likely to be something firmly rooted in this world to which they have ascribed eternal significance – as in the case of football supporters whose last wish is to have their ashes scattered as near as possible to their team's sacred ground. This is the language which they themselves would certainly use. As Edward Bailey says, their devotion to a value which they believe to be transcendent may be as self-less and profound as that of any person who explicitly identifies themselves as religious. Bailey describes this kind of religious awareness as "commitment to the human" (2001). It is this kind of commitment to a 'trans-human humaneness', a sense of value shared at the deepest (or highest) level by all human beings which opens our need to find refuge for ourselves into a determination to provide it for others too, so that it develops into a culture of sharing rather than an empathic impulse felt at the individual level.

Thus a culture which officially discounts metaphysics is nevertheless deeply beholden to metaphysically minded people, and to the fact that unseen, unquantifiable sources of support continue to make their presence felt whether or not their presence is acknowledged or their nature identified. In many cases to be too explicit about religious belief may actually have a negative effect on those whose experience of organised religion has proved alienating in the past, so that, if the intention is to provide refuge and a sense of security, the demands of mission must give way before those of pastoral care and religious awareness be communicated implicitly rather than explicitly.

Much humanitarian psychotherapy is a response to the need for psychologically wounded people to feel that they are loved and cared for, that they are in fact secure. This response concentrates on the fostering of a healing encounter between therapist and client. So far as it concentrates on relationship it chimes with Martin Buber's teaching about God's presence "between man and man" and the origins of humanist psychotherapy point to a good deal of contact between Buber and Carl Rogers. The therapeutic relationship remains at the centre of almost all psychotherapies.

> It is perhaps the focus on the quality of the relationship that is particularly significant, as there is a growing awareness across a range of professions that helping involves more than the application of specific treatment regimes in a standardised fashion. Increasingly it is perceived as an interaction between two people in which a key factor is the quality of their relationship ... whatever the skill, this is best employed within the framework of a relationship characterised by Rogers (1951) as containing the core personal dispositions of empathy, acceptance and congruence. (Strawbridge & Woolfe 2003:4)

These three therapeutic factors belong together because each of them implies the other two. Without opening oneself to what the other person is experiencing, I cannot really accept them into a genuine relationship; on the other hand my acceptance of them is of no real value to them if I am refusing to be honest about myself. The two-way agreement to meet each other as we are depends on clearing a space for mutual acceptance. The purpose of the therapist's three-fold acceptance of the client is via the relationship which grows between them, to encourage each client to have the same degree of regard for themselves as the therapist has for them.

> As time has gone by we (Rogers) have come to put increasing stress upon the 'client-centredness' of the relationship because it is more effective the more completely the counsellor concentrates upon trying to understand the client *as the client seems to himself.* (1951:10)

Other approaches concentrate more on the interpretation of the client's mental life and take a more didactic stance within the therapist-client interaction, but this central stress on establishing a relationship, the terms of which are understood and accepted by both parties – or in the case of group therapy, all parties – remains fundamental to all kinds of psychotherapy. What Rogers is saying here any practitioner will endorse: the client must be allowed to feel at home in a relationship based upon the latter's acceptance of the person the former feels himself to be. The therapy only starts when the client feels a measure of personal safety. Historically speaking psychotherapy of this kind originated in attempts to rebuild minds made dysfunctional by horrific experiences of actual combat: first a place of safety, then the first faltering steps towards a kind of sense. Again it was a sense of a situation safe enough for experiences which are intensely personal, and would under normal conditions be kept to oneself, to be shared with another person. From the start psychotherapy has concentrated on this action of sharing, most vividly demonstrated in forms of group therapy such as group analysis. S.H. Foulkes described the origins of such work with groups of shell-shocked soldiers seeking refuge from the terrors induced by armed conflict:

> Every aspect of the patient's life (at the Northfield Army Neurosis Centre) was turned to their therapeutic use. Everything that he did became treatment in the best sense of the word. Forming an essential therapeutic link in the rehabilitation was group therapy in its many varied aspects. (1957:43, 44)

People who seek refuge are looking for a place of safety and peace. It would be closer to the truth to say that they are seeking something which they themselves will find safe and peaceful. Whatever is offered, then, requires a response. This in itself may well be a problem to those concerned because of things which get in the way of responsiveness, particularly in the case of emotionally wounded people, whose suffering has made it hard for them to form relationships with others. Offers of love and friendship are turned down as the idea of love has been made aversive through its association with punishment, and friendship has turned out to be an inadequate support in times of trouble. Human relationship turns out to be not nearly as straightforward as we seem to assume it to be. It is not and cannot in fact ever be simply two persons who know each other living in a condition of mutual acceptance. Relationship is problematic 'from the word go', and not only for those who have been unfortunate enough to have been wounded by its failure, but for those who believe themselves to have no difficulties in this direction and find it easy to get on with people. We all have ways of keeping others at a distance and we all use them for most of the time. The ease with which I deal with you in the relationship we share actually comes not so much from my own generosity and open-heartedness as from that fact that you happen to fit so well (so neatly?) into my plan of the world, confirming by your presence its acceptability as a way of making sense of people and things.

In fact it takes a particular kind of courage both to accept refuge and to give it. This is because relationship itself is a self-protective action. What is called for is a kind of involvement which is tough enough to include ambiguities and possesses the necessary resilience to overcome the protective mechanisms we include automatically in our ordinary idea of relationship. It requires an extraordinary love.

This is not to devalue relationship, but to try to understand the way it works. True relationship represents the triumph of love over self-protectiveness; it involves nurturing in the courage to be protected by others and to reach out to protect them in return – to lose and be lost, and gain and be gained, all this happening in quick succession as awareness oscillates between the safety and the danger implied within the project of giving oneself and yet somehow remaining safe enough to go on giving.

(d)   Refuge and Relationship

"Every true experience is the experience of encounter," says Dewey (1934:22). Encounters, however, may be frightening or even aversive. The courage to be in relationship with others and the courage to be oneself are, of course, the same courage, the second being dependent on the first. At a purely cognitive level, the action of trying to make sense of the world involves risk: we may either make too little sense and be less successful in our efforts to control what we perceive, or too much and lose our sense of being any kind of free agent in the business of sense-making. In either case the dynamic process of learning to make sense will be interrupted by factors over which we have little or no control, the presence in our world of other sense-makers in particular. However neither the problem itself nor its solution can be regarded as simply one of developing the ability to strike a balance between assimilation to and accommodation of new information. This is a problem of living, not simply thinking. Developing children gain the courage to deal with the world as gift rather than argument because they themselves have received it in this way. John Bowlby's (1980) investigations into the depth of connection between the child and its mother pointed to a connectedness of exchanged love which is the principal source of the child's ability to encounter the world. The courage required to set sail on the ocean of relatedness to whatever is not ourselves stems from the experience of an attachment which is so secure, so 'safe', that any dangers which face us later on may be tackled from a position of basic confidence. In other words, the most important thing we ever learn is the ability to see ourselves loved and therefore fundamentally lovable. In the opposition between inner and outer, courage and fear, the balance is held by love.

The philosophical anthropology of Martin Buber regards human relationships in the same way, as the balance held between courage and fear. We are called out of ourselves by the fellow feeling which exists between us and another, and drawn back into our protective shell for fear that this same other will engulf us. In our courage lies our annihilation; and yet our need for engagement is such that we are driven ceaselessly to repeat the exercise. To be in relationship, says Buber, is to be always retreating in order to be always advancing. It is the moment of contact, of 'I-Thou' which gives life and encouragement, but the need to retreat from the challenge of this kind of exposure also contributes to relationship as we reflect upon what is happening and to plan new encounters under the temporary protection offered by 'I-It'. These, according to Buber, are the dynamics of relationship as it functions between and among human beings, courage and self-protectiveness contributing equally to what takes place between.

All the same, the fact that relationship prevails shows the balance to be an unequal one, as indeed it is bound to be so long as the retreat into impersonality makes the personal more attractive; and this is bound to be the case because the personal, however much it threatens us, is nevertheless the source of life. As Buber puts it, "without 'It' man cannot live. But he who lives with 'It' alone is not a man" (1966:34). 'It' provides refuge for 'Thou' for 'It', but the refuge provided by 'Thou' is healing contact with life itself.

It turns out, then, that the answer to the woundedness which cries out for refuge of a kind which we are able to accept and invest in, lies in the discovery that we are loved in a way which is total and overpowering; grasped, swept up and held by love. This love is primal as in a parent's love for a child, and eternal as God's love for creation. The aim of pastoral care is to mediate this awareness.

(e)   Refuge and Religion

"The Lord is our refuge and strength, a very present help in trouble" (Ps. 46). Religious people regard God as their most important source of protection against every kind of evil which may assail them. In religious thought, the divine person or influence is protective and restorative by definition. "From whence cometh my help," the Psalmist asks, and his reply is direct and unconditional: "My help cometh from the Lord" (Ps. 121). The other great religions of the world echo the same confidence: "Even though I have gone astray I am thy child, O God: thou art my father and mother" (Sikh prayer). All the same it is never an easy kind of confidence; we prefer our own way of being safe to the overshadowing of God's wing. Instead of God-as-he-has-shown-himself-to-be we turn for shelter to a God of our own, construing a substitute 'god-system' which because it is something we have made; an 'I-It' presents us with every divine requirement and no divine wherewithal to perform any of them. No wonder the place of refreshment, light and peace is experienced as the presence of rules which cannot be kept, and deliverance and renewal are seen as guilt and oppression. But just as human relationships entail a surrender which is mutual so does our relationship with God. If he comes to meet us we must discover the courage to respond by abandoning all our painstaking effort to show ourselves worthy of his protection and to accept his deliverance as a living fact of our life, a fait accompli not some kind of provisional offer.

These are matters of great relevance to the practice of pastoral care. Somehow the experience of God as harsh taskmaster and cruel judge has to be banished from the awareness of those who seek relief from anxiety and help in bearing the burdens of life. Religion everywhere is united in assuring us that it is God who takes the initiative, for such is the nature of divinity.

> Merciful God, you have prepared for those who love you
> such good things as pass our understanding. Pour into
> our hearts such love towards you that we, loving you in
> all things and above all things, may obtain your promises.
> (Christian)

The promises of God are founded upon his willingness to help us to respond to him. What God requires of us he enables us to perform. Just as he cannot do this unless he is God, he cannot be God for us unless he does it. This is the awareness of God who protects us not because of our faith but because of our need. It is this understanding which pastoral care calls upon to comfort and reassure those who believe in a God who rejects them, either because he does not really know them or because they feel he knows them too well; or simply because faith lies beyond their grasp. This last applies as much to God's officials as to God himself. The most obvious casualties of religion are the victims of religious or sectarian conflict, but the wounding may be, and often is, more subtle that this. Where people are psychologically threatened by religious teaching, it may not be so much that they themselves have got the message about God wrong but that they have been given the wrong message. In fact they have been much better taught about demands than assurances, so that the conditional nature of acceptance has become firmly implanted in their awareness. After all, human acceptance is always a conditional affair.

Divine acceptance, the invitation to encounter God, is theology notwithstanding, unconditional; and this is the face of God which concerns pastoral care. Questions about personal worthiness follow this revelation and must not be allowed to obscure it and occlude its radiance. Its purpose is to attract not to repel, and to do so within the context of human need. In the context of our religious awareness need is felt as a falling away from perfection and a desire to manufacture it in some way in order to prove acceptable to God. So long as we persist in seeing it this way the revelation continues to be occluded, for the true meaning of our failure to achieve our own perfection is to turn us towards God's success in drawing us into his. This is something which can only be taken on trust, however, because it is not the way we are used to dealing with our problems of relationship. It is, as Tillich says, a matter of faith – accepting acceptance because I am unacceptable (1962:Ch.VI).

But what about offers of help which, once accepted, themselves turn out to be unacceptable? Not every island on which we make landfall is able to support life. It may appear to be fertile and welcoming when we glimpse it on the horizon and then turn out to be not what we had hoped for or could live with. To perish from exposure on barren rock is as bad as drowning, particularly if the island appeared to be fertile and welcoming. The imagery of desert islands is, like that of deserts themselves, directed towards ideas of trial and feats of endurance. Those who seek refuge from their inner desolation are not going to be comforted by judgement posing as acceptance. The testimony of people who have turned to religion in order to find solace and healing only to discover that its practitioners actually equate suffering with virtue, an attitude of mind which is only too easily projected onto others – for their own good, of course ...

This is the most important lesson of all for pastoral care to learn: that other people are where they are and not where we like them to be. Not where we find ourselves. We may have well-developed theories, which amount to personal conviction about what is best in the long run for someone in trouble 'having dealt with this kind of thing before' or even 'been there ourselves' – the latter being the easiest mistake to make and perhaps the most dangerous one too. People who are seeking refuge are likely to misconstrue our intentions if they are not immediately made aware of our efforts to make them feel better: 'I know that you are only doing this for my own good' is not likely to be their immediate reaction to the kind of reception which refuses to show personal involvement which is non-judgemental, spontaneous and obviously heartfelt. The experience of many seekers after acceptance has reminded them more of a rocky shoreline than a beach reaching out to rescue and welcome them.

- When I say to my priest that I can't seem to find any peace of mind, he says I should go to mass more often. But I do, I do.
- The pastor says that being depressed proves I haven't enough faith.
- I went to ask the Reverend what I could possibly do, and he said I should make an appointment with his secretary. I know he's very busy, but I felt let down at the time.
- When folk say that God is love, I always think of my knees red and raw from washing the corridor at the convent.
- The people in the church I go to say they can't keep on trying to help. I think they think I do it on purpose.

The human need for refuge is vividly and unforgettably expressed in the symbolism of islands. The work of pastoral care is to make sure the image is authentic and the experience of acceptance genuine. The search for refuge is a fundamental theme in psychotherapy, and because of the need for distance, of a place set apart from presences which have become oppressive and intrusive, island imagery is implied even when it is not actually spelled out. I asked a psychotherapist to describe this from her own experience of clients searching for islands of safety within the ocean of life:

Refuges: Ann Rew

I have been asked to write a few words on refuge. From a personal perspective my need for refuge was important. It was a place inside of me – a place where I could not be reached or touched.

It needed to be a quiet and still place that was calm and peaceful. The problem was that the place I built was empty of people so it was also isolating and lonely, which was indicative of my relationship with me at the time. However it was also a safe refuge from the outside.

I became more aware of where I had put that core essence of me. I decided to build a place that was more in keeping with who I felt I am at this moment.

I enter my refuge by walking down a tree-lined lane, almost like a tunnel of green with a springtime sun glinting through the leaves. The only sounds are the gentle rushing of the leaves from the wind and the birds and insects around about.

As I walk down this lane I can feel the sense of peace and calm rising in me. The walk can be as long or as short as I choose. At the end of the lane I move into an enclosed area that is as big as I choose to make it. I have placed in this area a grotto overgrown with greenery, running water in the form of a cascade and stream that feeds a pool. Sometimes I visualise animals as well, depending on my wish and my mood.

I visualise myself in clothes that are comfortable and I am usually bare-footed as I wander round on the grass or sit and drink in the atmosphere. Whilst there I am also able to think about things that are troubling me and that I need to resolve. Also whilst there I meditate and rest.

I wondered whether I could use this same technique within my work as a therapist, enabling my clients to explore their inner world and the ways that they protect themselves through building refuges, have an internal world.

(a)

The first one to come to mind, whom I shall call John in order to maintain confidentiality. When I asked him where he felt himself to be hiding within he responded by describing a tunnel. He went into great detail, how black it was, the bars at each end which stopped people from getting in but also stopped him from getting out. His refuge was not only a protection but also a prison.

We began exploring his tunnel and what it gained him – protection and safety. Also what he lost – connection, relationship and intimacy. I asked permission to enter his tunnel, which surprised him. He wondered why I would want to. This, I felt, was telling how he felt about himself – a belief that no-one would want to be near him and maybe he was afraid to let anyone get close just in case his negative belief about himself was shown to be correct. We sat quietly in his tunnel for quite a few sessions as he shared his history, his life, his feelings and beliefs about himself.

As the trust grew and the relationship deepened we began to explore the possibility of finding a way out of the tunnel together, with the proviso that he could re-enter it whenever he felt he needed to, when threatened or scared.

I used my own imagination to create a way of unlocking the bars at one end. What I used was the power of love. We were able to melt them and walk out together and so we sat side by side just the other side of the opening to the tunnel.

We slowly began the exploration of the world around him and he decided that it was not scary, this outside world. We also explored the option of building another refuge within. The one he built was full of open spaces and filled with a sense of freedom. When the client came to the end of his therapy he was able to 'walk off down the road, because he was going fishing'.

(b)

Another client called Susan described her refuge in a different way. She talked of a huge mansion in grounds with her inside. I asked how it would feel for her if I knocked on the front door and asked permission to enter.

Susan was given the choice of opening the door or not. The relationship between us enabled her to open the door.

As I walked in Susan described what was there – it was a large hallway with many open rooms leading off from the hallway. None of these rooms had any doors so anyone who entered the mansion could see and enter these rooms. As we moved slowly deeper into the mansion the rooms began to have doors but open – the sense of freedom to roam within this refuge felt strong to me.

However as we travelled deeper the doors began to close. For some reason I just acknowledged that they were closed but did not attempt to open any. I felt it important to continue the journey deeper into the mansion. The doors got fewer and these were locked till finally we arrived at this one door which was locked, bolted and chained.

We sat down outside this door and explored why it had so much security and what might be on the other side of the door. We slowly began to remove the chains and then the bolts and unlock the door but I did not open the door. I felt it was important that Susan was the one to open the door and eventually she did.

What I found was a small child sitting in the dark, frightened and scared, cold and alone, looking at me.

I sat quietly at the entrance to the door for a while, just smiling at the child. Susan and I explored how that felt for her – scary. I began gently speaking to Susan/child, reassuring her. I had no wish to frighten someone who had taken so much trouble to protect themselves in their refuge.

It took quite a few sessions before I was able to enter the room and sit beside Susan and only then did we talk about leaving the room. During this time we explored having a window and looking out or opening the window and letting the fresh air in.

Susan decided that it was OK to move out of the room and we slowly walked out hand in hand. We moved out into the garden and sat in the sun. We often went back into the mansion and explored what we found behind those shut and locked rooms. But always the session ended with us outside in the sun sitting together.

Susan went on to build another refuge that was more open and free.

Another client described themselves as a balloon and that they hated balloons. It felt to me as if their place of refuge was in a place of hatred with no space and no escape.

The first thing I did was to explore the possibility of changing the balloon into a bubble. Their main fear was that I would burst it so we explored ways of protecting it. I also explored with this client the description of this bubble and we decided that it was full of rainbows. The reason that I wanted to change the balloon into a bubble was so that I could see her.

We worked on the bubble, slowly expanding it so that we could give her a sense of space. I asked what she would like in her bubble. It began with a chair so that she could sit down, which she did and I sat down outside the bubble. We explored the chair, what type etc. – it needed to be comfortable for her. The client then added a lamp over the chair so that she could be seen better and to see what she was reading. Slowly we added other furniture – a desk, shelves for books etc. The most important thing the client was able to add was a door so that she could come or go as she pleased.

As we worked on this image of her refuge there seemed to be a parallel process at work in reality. The client was slowly beginning to take over a room in her own home and make it her own. She turned her imagined refuge into a reality, a place to retreat to.

(c)

A third client felt very unsafe and exposed so we explored what they would need to be safe. Firstly I explored how they saw themselves and they spoke of being a 'Muggle' – they had been reading the Harry Potter books. I challenged this and we worked on the magic that was in them. Once they had come to terms with this concept and accepted it, it became easier to look for a safe place within them using their 'magic' powers.

The client began by building an island with a mountain on it. They spent some time talking about it and even went on to paint it. It felt a bit bare so I invited them to think about what they would like on their island.

They talked of plants of all different sorts and trees, places of shelter from the sun when it got too hot. There were flowers and fruits to eat. They added butterflies and birds as well. Sights and sounds were beginning to populate the island.

We explored where on the island they would like to stay – close to the sea but not too close. They built a house and began to furnish it with a comfortable bed and other furniture.

Once they had this 'place' to go to and rest from the world I asked who would they like to visit them on the island and how would they get there –

no airplanes were allowed so it was by boat and they needed to know that they could ask the visitor to leave whenever they wanted them to.

I felt that the trust between us was evidenced when I got invited to go to the island.

We sat on that island many times together and they felt safe and able to explore the issues in their own safe place. They had control over things in that safe refuge and they found that they could be themselves.

From this safe refuge they began to take what they had learned out into the wider world.

CHAPTER 8
Time Out

(a)   Profit and Loss

> Most men, even in this comparatively free country, through
> mere ignorance and mistake, are so occupied with the
> factitious cares and superficially coarse labors of life that its
> finer fruits cannot be plucked by them. Their fingers, from
> excessive toil, are too clumsy and tremble too much for
> that. (*Walden*, Henry Thoreau)

Henry Thoreau said men and women are working too hard. Like
Wordsworth, he complained that

> The world is too much with us. Late and soon
> Getting and spending, we lay waste our powers. (*Sonnet*)

Both men wrote in the nineteenth century; their work might be considered
to span the Romantic movement in western literature. However some of
the things they both say are quite definitely realistic. In the nineteenth
century people did work too hard, either for themselves or someone else,
which is a less direct and usually less financially rewarding way of doing
the same thing. The same is true today, of course; we use our "comparative
freedom" to work as hard as we can "getting and spending". Even if we
ourselves can conceive of a time when we may feel we have enough of the
commodities and social privileges which lead us to work ever harder, we

live in an economic system which has never had enough; which can only preserve itself by never having had enough, in fact.

From time to time, certainly, people decide to take Thoreau's option – it is still sometimes an option – and 'opt out of the rat race' by taking up an occupation which will give them more time to enjoy life at the cost of having less money to enjoy it with; but most people are too tightly enmeshed in what is, after all, the socially required way of living to do this, even if they wanted to (and their eagerness to take advantage of holidays as a means of escape shows that they do, or at least part of them does).

It could reasonably be argued that restrictions on personal space are growing increasingly intense as the economic imperative becomes more and more dominant and its expression cruder and less humane. In the nineteenth century the growth of the trades unions served as a reminder of workers' need to be considered as people as well as providers of capital, but latterly their voice has carried less weight while the demand for ever-increasing profits, work quotas which automatically get higher as production increases, has invaded sections of society whose work ethos was qualitative as well as quantitative; where the state of mind of employees was taken into account as part of the profit/loss balance.

Certainly achievable tasks can be tedious if there are too many of them and they are too obviously achievable. We need a degree of challenge to stave off boredom, particularly if our job is repetitious and consequently uninspiring. Perhaps what we most need in order to feel ourselves alert and alive is an ongoing series of achievable goals, so that we are always being challenged and always rewarded. The greater the challenge, the more unexpected the success which rewards it – and this is what gives us most satisfaction. We would like to be in a position to arrange our own lives so that we have not only enjoyable things to do but rewarding problems to solve … "The daily round, the common task Should furnish all we ought to ask", says the hymn writer. Unfortunately, however, it often fails to do so. First it falls far short of what we ourselves would have chosen, such as our need for a degree of stimulation and variety in what we do. Second, because we have not actually chosen to do it, we find ourselves envying those who have had some say in what they end up doing; or perhaps we did choose it and have only ourselves to blame. Third, it may simply be an unpleasant job in itself, one which no-one would do for anything except the money, and a lot of jobs are in fact like that.

Obviously there are very many reasons for feeling discontented with the job we do. Equally obviously because, for most of our life, we work to earn a living and not just to occupy our time, we find it impossible simply to stop working, throw up our job and live a more leisurely life without having to do what other people, or we ourselves, tell us to do. Wanting to be our own boss is certainly one of the most important reasons for finding the job we have to do unsatisfactory; and yet we know well that we ourselves can be the most demanding task-masters of all. All the same we would like the opportunity to give it a try – hence the popularity of novels and television programmes about men and women who suddenly quit their secure, well-paid jobs to become basket-weavers or beachcombers. The call of the Lake Isle is a powerful one, promising as it does a simpler life, an easier job, a happy and carefree heart:

> I will arise and go now, and go to Innisfree,
> And a small cabin build there, of clay and wattles made.
> Nine bean-rows will I have there, a hive for the honey-bee
> And live alone in the bee-loud glade. (*The Lake Isle of Innisfree* 1893)

Yeats's vision is not feasible for most of us. It wasn't for him either of course. That is its power to involve us in a succession of imaginary escapes from reality which actually affect our ordinary lives. The holidays we take are more adventurous because we identify distance with romance – the further from home we travel, the more likely we are to achieve our aim to 'get away from it all'.

In this way poetic imagination confronts a more prosaic reality and is not defeated by it, as the island fantasy survives repeated experiences of actual tourist hideaways which have notoriously failed to live up to the dream. If work can never be done well enough leisure becomes more precious, and the nature of leisure changes. There are no rows of beans on our dream island and certainly no bees! In fact there will be very little work of any kind at all, certainly nothing tedious or back-breaking.

But do we really want to be alone, in charge and idle? Yeats longed for solitude; for Alexander Selkirk, to whom it actually happened, being "Monarch of all I survey" was no substitute for never being able to "hear the sacred music of speech". Prospero, who like Caesar in Rome "doth bestride the narrow world" of his island "like a Colossus", takes good care not to be entirely alone there. What the two islands, Yeats's and Prospero's, have in common is the absence of hard work to be carried out by their tenants. Yeats's beans are grown with pleasure for the joy of growing things;

while on Prospero's isle the domestic arrangements are accommodated within the magical and agriculture is 'for amusement only'.

> Enter certain Reapers, properly habited; they join with the nymphs in a graceful dance. (Act IV sc.1)

The face of his island which Prospero shows to the young lovers is that of a haven from stress and anxiety, a place of poetry and peace of mind and body in which the rigours of life have been left behind. It is not work itself which is the problem, but work which has got out of control; work, or absence of work, which somehow deprives us of our sense of freedom to be a worker. Prospero himself has worked very hard without ever becoming the slave of his own labours, and he is keen to let us know it:

> this rough magic
> I here abjure ... I'll break my staff,
> Bury it certain fathoms in the earth
> And deeper than did ever plummet sound,
> I'll drown my book. (Act V sc.1)

What, we are left wondering, will he find to do now?

(b)   Working or not working?

Hard, boring, incessantly demanding though it may sometimes be, work of some kind or other is vitally important for our spiritual and psychological well-being. This, however, is to change the meaning of the word so that it applies to concentrated or task-orientated activity of any kind and not simply to punitive toil implied by The Book of Genesis. The lifetime of hard labour to which Adam and Eve were sentenced remains near the surface of the way we think about work, so much so that it is quite usual to find people apologising for the way they spend their time – actually doing something which they find enjoyable and satisfying. If you like doing it, it's simply a hobby. What makes genuine work is if you have to do it and carry on doing it whatever you feel like; if and when it begins to cause you some kind of pain, then you can begin to call it work.

The world outside Eden requires work. It draws work from us. Without work of some kind we lose the sense of engagement with our own reality. Work is the evidence we call upon to assure ourselves that we belong in the world. This is not necessarily paid work, but it is work nonetheless;

we know it is because we go on doing it even though it has become arduous, even though nobody is forcing us to do it. Our minds search for solutions which involve our bodies. Religious experience simply makes us eager to work harder as joy is more creative than apathy. At this level the discomfort attached to work gives rise to genuine satisfaction, as work for a transcendent purpose is the most fulfilling of all.

Not only religious people find work fulfilling, however. The pleasure derived from working at something felt to be worthwhile is characteristic of the human species, outweighing fatigue, frustration and failure. At a neurological level we must make contact or deteriorate into madness; and for us, to make contact is to work, whether our employment be artificial intelligence or the opus dei, or quite simply making sure that the place where we live is reasonably clean and tidy. There is definitely a psycho-neurological connection here between work and anxiety. Housework is typified in popular culture as boring, arduous, repetitive, a load which everybody would agree (say the advertisers) always needs to be lightened (advertisers don't go in for 'sometimes'). However it is also a cliché that working round the house relieves anxiety – "So I got on with the ironing; there was a load of it and it took my mind off things". Just as some work increases anxiety – Philip, for instance – so some can be used to calm ourselves down. Cognitive Behavioural Psychology (CBT) starts out from Epictetus's claim that "People are not disturbed by things but by the view they take of them". Our feelings are governed by the way we assess the situation: if we think there is too much housework we become anxious and the task itself becomes harder for us to accomplish because of the way we feel; but if we think we will be able to cope with the amount or decide only to tackle part of it, then we can accomplish it without feeling upset by it.

What is more to the point, we may even enjoy doing it, as after all his adventures Voltaire's Candide returns, with relief to "dig the garden". The same job under different circumstances gives rise to feelings which are entirely different. Quite ordinary jobs like digging the garden can sometimes help us to feel better when we have been over-stimulated, over-anxious. If Candide had been a gardening expert, digging the garden would probably have increased his anxiety; after all, he had been a long time away from it and the weeds would have got badly out of hand. However under the circumstances a normal, straightforward job like digging was ideal. He needed to do something and the garden was out there, waiting to be dug …

Too much excitement leaves us feeling the need for something steady and unexciting. On the other hand too little activity leaves us longing for occupation of any kind. Just as work keeps us steady, so it keeps us going. Most of us, most of the time would prefer to have to work too hard than not to have to work at all. We may not want to work but we know we need to, and not only for financial reasons either. We have a sense that having a job to do is the proper condition for human beings to be in, that rest is necessary and should be enjoyed – but then, so should work. Never wanting to work at all is immoral and pathological. Work is and always will be part of life for human beings. It is something we have to make the best of.

If this is how we feel, it is hard to sustain the biblical teaching of work as a punishment, or the Puritan assumption that it is a compulsory response to our being forgiven; work is too necessary for our happiness, too benign in fact, to be regarded simply as a necessary evil, a price to be paid; and yet, through its use as a way of structuring human society it can be the source of very real pain. We judge people by the kinds of work they do and our judgements control their lives to a greater extent than we like to imagine.

Lindsays's story is an example because it illustrates both the positive and negative aspects of work:

Lindsay is thirty and has never had a job of any kind. She lives in her own flat which is in the next road to her parents' house in a well-to-do part of Leicester. When she was a child she had rheumatic fever, and although she recovered from this a long time ago, her parents, particularly her father, still regard her as a vulnerable little girl, taking her away from school before she could take her final exams "because of the strain of having to study too hard". Lindsay managed to get into college; again her parents' protectiveness led to her failing to complete the course. A friendly girl with an attractive personality, she had made several friends at school, all of whom had by now gained university degrees and launched out into various jobs. Lindsay saw herself as someone who "even with her parents' help" couldn't manage even to get properly started on a career. Obviously she was an inadequate person and would go on being one. I suggested that she should try the Open University and this turned out to be a good idea as she did very well. The fact that she secured a good degree "without even having to go away to college" impressed her with a sense of her own capabilities. Unfortunately, however, by the time this happened her friends were "either starting families or getting on in their jobs" – so again Lindsay felt that she was behind and could never draw level. (She also had real doubts as to whether studying at home, which she had been doing as an OU student, really counted anyway ...)

(c)   Time to Play

If our relationship with work is a problematic one, our feelings about play are even more so. It is only under certain well-defined circumstances that adults will consent to play at all. For many people in our culture playing is something done by others on our behalf; or rather, we ourselves play by becoming involved in other people's work activity – in dance, dramatic presentation, or above all, spectator sports. In such cases the playing is a function of the distance between ourselves and the hard work being done by others for our pleasure. This is not to say that we never do these things ourselves, but that on the whole we seem to prefer to watch others doing them on our behalf. We ourselves don't actually play, not for pleasure.

Not if we are grown up, that is. Playing spontaneously simply because we feel like it is a sign of childishness, of not being properly grown up. And yet it is very basic to us, as fundamental to our being human as work. Not that we think it is anything like so important. It is not in the nature of playing that we should, of course; if work maintains the fabric of public reality, play is a release from its demands. There would be no need for play if work were not intrinsically more demanding, for who needs a rest from pressures which can simply be ignored? All the same, this tendency to underplay this side of life must be countered because we need it so much for its vital contribution to the world of work, a world in which our cognitive-emotional as well as our organic life depends.

Playing is a vital holiday from our involvement in the work of the world. When we play, says Alida Gersie,

> we loosen our connection with experienced reality, for it is
> difficult to play when we are preoccupied with the events
> of our daily life. The exploration of alternatives which
> is inherent to play demands centred freedom. This is a
> freedom which comes from the belief that the world will
> continue to exist while we absent ourselves to embark upon
> a journey of inner and outer discovery. (1987:46)

Playing is expected of children and they live up to the expectation. When they are deprived of the opportunity to make this "voyage of inner and outer discovery", the effect upon their cognitive-emotional development is striking because of the interaction which takes place between environmental stimulation and psychological growth and development. Children, of course, play for fun; indeed, it is hard to stop a young child playing, "exploring alternatives" to whatever may be presented to them. Adults somehow appear to have lost the knack. Having to adjust to real work in the real world has been so traumatic to the urge to play that they prefer not to join in anything even vaguely 'childish' (*i.e.* imaginative), except in the privacy of their own homes and with their own children, a setting emotionally secure enough to provide what Gersie calls "centred freedom".

Not all children can share in this way, of course. Anne Cattenach describes the 'play therapy' she carries out with children whose privacy has been invaded in disastrous ways by adults:

> In order to help the child feel that play with me is separate
> from what goes on in the house the rest of the time, I carry
> my separate and safe place with me. This is the 'Blue Mat'
> of magical significance … I explain to the child that this is
> the mat on which we sit and play … when we fold up the
> mat at the end of the time we can leave what we have done
> in play behind and start afresh the next time. (1992:138)

Obviously it is far from easy to persuade emotionally wounded children to play unselfconsciously with someone who is, to begin with, a complete stranger, although Cattenach points out that this may be one of the chief reasons why her approach actually works: it offers the possibility of new beginnings. With adults, however, it can be just as hard because playing imaginative games – or being seen to be playing them – is something they have 'grown out of'. All the same it remains a possibility, as dramatherapy demonstrates.

Dramatherapists approach the problem of getting people to play in a very direct way. They have to, because playing games together is a sure way of unlocking peoples' imaginations; and it is on imaginative sharing that dramatherapy depends: shared imagination is its therapeutic medium. Consequently the first third of a dramatherapy session takes the form of an extended game, the serious work of the session arriving later on:

Under the direction of the therapist, a group of people

stand in a circle. After some physical 'warm-up' exercises, games are played to help people feel that they are members of the group so that they become less self-conscious. This part of the proceedings usually begins in an atmosphere of wariness, with nobody knowing what will happen next, and ends with a certain amount of hilarity, as people express their relief at finding they are, after all, enjoying themselves. (Grainger 1995:8, adapted)

We all stood in a circle and said our names. You always have to do this every group you're in and you more or less get to take it for granted. This time we did something a bit different though. You were allowed to say someone else's name, either the person standing on your right or the one on your left. (This was a bit difficult at first, if you couldn't remember their name so you had to wait until the person next to them said it – or you could ask them, of course, but you didn't want to show that you'd forgotten their name. This was the only name you were allowed to say, the person on your right or the one on your left, which meant that they could say *your* name and you had to keep saying their name, and they saying yours until one of you gave in and said the name of the person on the other side. It sounds awful, but it was actually a lot of fun, trying to get them to give in without giving in yourself, fighting a verbal battle you could get out of at any time by turning the other way and saying the name of the person on your other side – who could then throw your name back at you etc. Sometimes this went on for a long time among the three people involved until one of them gave in and let things move on round the circle. It was a kind of acting game, as people tried out a whole range of ways of saying someone's name in order to get them to give in and turn in the other direction. Above all, it was funny so that you felt tired out with laughing, and perfectly willing to give your whole attention to the quieter and more serious things which were to follow … (A dramatherapy group member)

Not everyone is as enthusiastic as this, and the "serious part" is certainly more challenging as the group explores ways of using imagination to penetrate the self-protective shell which surrounds their experience of ordinary life. But before they turn to anything so deeply personal, they have already broken down the barrier of ordinary self-consciousness which made some of them wonder why they had said they would take part to begin with, and the rest feel clumsy and inadequate, out of place in a group of any kind. Playing a game together breaks down barriers, even if you haven't chosen to play it yourself; learning how to do it is a satisfying process so long as it's not too complicated. Even getting it wrong may be rewarding in a situation where everyone else is doing the same thing and people are laughing in an appreciative way, with you and not at you.

This kind of game obviously has a serious purpose in any kind of group work because it helps build an awareness of belonging together and yet gaining a special personal identity as a group member, someone actively contributing as themselves. The way in which social and individual identity co-inhere is clearly demonstrated in the activity of playing games with other people and the way in which we summon up imaginary personages to take part with us in the games we play by ourselves. Games have a deep seriousness as experiences of relationship. Perhaps this is why we treat them as a special way of behaving. Special is exactly what they are, because relationship is what we are afraid of except under very particular circumstances. The straightforward presentation of who we know ourselves to be is alarming simply because it is unprotected. "Don't worry, it's just a game" sets our mind at rest, and we are at least willing to work together as ourselves – which is why games are so important.

Put like this we can see that the distinction between work and play is not so complete and exclusive as it may have appeared to be. Playing is a kind of self-and-other-aware working – work which has been set free from the understanding we are used to having of it as a burden laid on ourselves as individuals – either a generic one attached to those living in our circumstances or a more personal one for which we ourselves should be held responsible. We may see ourselves as contributing to something wider and more important, but this is a theoretical idea not a fact of present experience. Games bring home our dependence on each other as a real fact, an experience within present reality, not some sort of idealistic reaching out after an impossible goal.

Religious faith brings idealistic goals nearer because it imbues them with spiritual presence, one that reaches out for embodiment in some kind of celebration of shared spiritual experience. This, again, is not actually playing – it is considered to be too serious for that – all the same it has the basic structure of a game in that it creates in its own world which it consciously distinguishes from any human activity other than itself; and it binds persons together in a shared task of self-revelation, albeit on a spiritual rather than a prosaic plane. The aim is to embark on a way of being related to the Other which will somehow be transferable to the conditions of daily living. Just as the hilarity of the name-game allowed the dramatherapy group to share at a quite serious level their own personal concerns, so the experience of surrendering to God in corporate worship affects the way we regard one another in our ordinary lives with greater awareness of our fellow men and women and a deeper need for honesty and mutuality.

Our experience of living within society is itself highly structured. Other people, if they are not relatives or friends, are 'strangers', 'foreigners', potential rivals to what we see ourselves enjoying. Our working life is divided up according to what Durkheim called "the division of labour" (1893), and we ourselves refer to as 'professionalism'. There are many inducements for people to 'keep themselves to themselves'. As remarked in Chapter One, we hesitate to come too close to people unless we know them very well. When we start to play, however, the differences between us cease to be alienating as we and they are bound by the same rules, which all the players accept and use as ways of expressing their own individuality. In the game framework individuals are valued because of their individuality, not in spite of it; we are not simply competitors but fellow competitors, competing fellows. We work and play at the same time, and the fact that we know we are playing makes us willing, sometimes, to work even harder.

For some religious people, of course, work of such a kind – work in the context of play – is not work at all. Within the Christian Protestant tradition for example, work is always fundamentally serious, being in fact the principal purpose of life. Max Weber describes a situation in which labour itself was to be valued as evidence of a redeemed condition in which human work is once more acceptable to God. As a result of this attitude

> The treatment of labour as a calling became as characteristic of the modern worker as the corresponding attitude towards acquisition of the business man. (1930:179)

Within the Judeo-Christian tradition work and play exist solely as opposites. The ability to use work productively and so create opportunities for even more work has been regarded as proof of personal salvation. Play, on the other hand, is an unfortunate hiatus in time that could have been spent working. It is used in a positive way to provide workers with the recreation necessary for them to be able to go on working. This is play viewed solely as entertainment, only valuable so long as it does not ever prove a distraction from the business of living.

(d)   Work and Art: Artwork

In fact work and play are by no means as polarised as this, and to treat them in this way is to fail to do justice to either. Art of all kinds provides us with evidence of how hard it is necessary for us to work in order to enshrine the spirit of play, of the creative imagination in real sounds, objects movements and words, so that these may spring back to life carrying with them something of their original freedom and spontaneity in order to produce an effect on the workaday world. Theatre demonstrates this in the most vivid way, possessing a power to change lives which has been recognised since Aristotle (Grainger 2006).

Theatre as work and play, imagination and reality, stands out in The Tempest with great clarity and immediacy, by demonstrating the contrast between Prospero's use of theatre as a way of providing his magical powers with a last fling before abandoning them for ever. (The Masque in Act IV is simple entertainment, delighting Miranda and Ferdinand with amazing feats of showmanship of the kind which "leave not a rack behind"). Prospero's real piece of theatre is, of course, the play itself. This is his work and it works with us, his audience at a deep psychological and spiritual level as a parable of catharsis and renewal.

At the end of the play Prospero asks us to work on his behalf so that he may now 'play'. The task he sets us is to pray for him. The ex-magician has lost his occupation; now he is dependent on our generosity in praying God to free him from the world he himself has laboured to create and to return him to reality. His power is all used up, but we can still work on his behalf from where we are:

> … my ending is despair
> Unless I be reliev'd by prayer …
> As you, from crimes would pardon'd be
> Let your indulgence set me free. (Act V sc.1)

Pastoral care can learn a great deal from this balance between structure and freedom in the exploration of experience. At the most obvious level it can learn ways of approaching serious subjects which, because they involve what we are accustomed to think of as 'the realities of life' (as if life itself were ashamed of its happier and more light-hearted aspects) and to be kept at arms' length in a friendlier fashion than they are usually dealt with. To give difficult subjects a dramatic shape is not to trivialise them but to make them personal in an acceptable way. What we are accustomed to doing is to talk solemnly about them in the role of expert in this particular painful area of life – sickness, mental illness, bereavement, dying – or if this is a religious talk, sin – preferably in the right sort of surroundings such as churches, classrooms or lecture halls. It is certainly true that these are subjects which should be broached. This, however, is not an effective way of sharing our understanding of them. It is too consciously solemn and signals its own seriousness in a way which has an over-distancing effect; the message we receive is that these things are about special aspects of reality concerned with lectures and sermons, the sphere of specialists of one kind of another. They are not about real people and real situations at all.

Actual drama turns out to be considerably closer to real life because of its power to involve us in experiences which are genuinely shared. Most importantly, by disclaiming its own reality it somehow manages to unlock ours. By coming clean about the distance between art and nature, work and play, drama allows us to share both. An example is the following workshop constructed as an alternative to the usual bible-study approach.

Adam and Eve in the Garden

You will need calm music,
paper for writing and drawing,
pencils, paints,
modeling clay etc.,

- Stand or sit in the most comfortable position and location you can find. If someone looks at you, smile at them but don't say anything. Just close your eyes and listen to the music.
- Move closer to the others so that you can all form a living chain by holding hands. Take turns to say your name and gently squeeze the hand(s) you are holding.

- Move into a circle and play a game of 'passing the squeeze' from one hand to another. (You can do this several times, passing the squeeze one way or the other around the circle. See how fast you can do it, then how slowly.)
- Read 'Adam and Eve in the Garden' (Genesis 2:4) as far as "for in the day that you eat of it, you shall die".
- Lead off round the room, the Leader describing all the places being passed through (e.g. imaginary rivers, forests, prairies, valleys, mountains etc). When the leader finds somewhere she or he would like to stay, they say that they like it and are going to stay there a while, and then hand over leadership to the next person in line. This goes on until everybody has found a place for themselves.
- Spend a moment or two thinking about The Tree of Life. Where would be the place to locate it? Write your suggestion on a piece of paper and leave it in the middle of the room. Choose someone to read the papers out; whichever part of the room has most votes, there the tree will stand.
- Sit around the Tree of Life. Take turns to say a few lines of poetry – anything at all which comes to mind – or sing a song you love, inviting the others to join in.
- Was there anything in the story which stood out for you personally? If there was, then share it with the others.
- Say the Lord's Prayer (or a prayer of another faith tradition), going on to thank God for the beauty and wonder of creation.
- Hold hands and say goodbye to one another.

CHAPTER 9
Bastions

A precious stone set in a silver sea
Which serves it in the office of a wall
Or as a moat defensive to a house. (*Richard III* Act II sc.1)

Sea and shore do not compromise; the former appears to move – never to stop moving in fact – but the rock stands still. The island itself is the very symbol of immovability, and people are rock-like in their resistance to change. Who you are is, we say, a matter of where you stand – and islands never move. Our vulnerability is proclaimed by our defensiveness, the ramparts we erect in order to impress people with our strength; the castles we build, the ditches we dig, our sophisticated electronic warning systems. We look strong and are weak, because our emotional defences are built on sand. Our ability to imagine ourselves stronger than we are renders the strongest minded of us the most vulnerable.

The surrounding sea acts as a defence, says Shakespeare; but seas shift and the tide lays bare what was previously hidden from view. The fortress is not as strong as it seemed; or its real strength lies hidden, masked by the sand. For human beings however it is a weakness which is covered over rather than strength. The notion of unacknowledged vulnerability, so clearly set out in the Gospel, is also a foundation stone for psychoanalysis. The conscious mind learns early on in its development to defend itself from the seductions of unconscious pleasure-seeking, and the more convincing its results seem to be the more they backfire on us in the form of neurotic symptoms (a fact explored at considerable length by Freud's daughter, Anna) and so make themselves felt.

A good deal of psychological effort goes into the business of avoiding the discomfort produced in us by the ways in which we find ourselves thinking and feeling. Just as, when our impulse is to fight we devote ourselves to avoiding fighting by learning how to be less aggressive, so we (and others when it suits them) manage to train ourselves systematically to deny or avoid our moments of gentleness and empathy, regarding them as inappropriate or just simply 'weak'. (After all, nobody wants people trampling over them, do they?) This stands out dramatically at those times when we are aware of danger in the shape of actual hostility aimed at us by others. In wartime, for example, a lot of effort goes into teaching ourselves to 'hate our enemies'; particularly if we are actual combatants whose job is to destroy other people by violent means. If this is so we will certainly put a great deal of effort into devising ways of doing this. The most effective way of all is the one used by old fashioned bayonet training, in which the awareness that our target is only a sack, not a real person makes it more possible to stick our bayonet through it. Similarly people are much easier to kill, and our inhibitions about killing them much less restricting, if we can convince ourselves that they are not really people at all.

The demand for life-giving contact, the relationship which keeps us all human and which we depend on in order to be people at all, persists despite our attempts to channel it in directions which we, or those who have power over us, find acceptable.

The young soldier referred to me for counselling had recently returned from a tour of duty in the Middle East, during which he and his comrade had been left behind in order to pass information on to their retreating unit. This involved their going to earth under very cramped conditions; so cramped in fact that his friend had literally been shot beneath him. The conditions in which they had lived and fought and one of them had died, had forged a close bond between them, one which occupied my client's thoughts and feelings to the exclusion of all else, so that nothing which had happened to him in the non-combatant 'peace-time' world seemed to make much sense. "The two worlds no longer seem to fit at all. This world just doesn't make sense."

He had been sent to me to see whether talking about what had happened would help him in any way. At first it certainly didn't seem to do so; until the hidden part of the story emerged and the grief-beneath-the-grief was exposed. This was the awareness which had been covered up by the trauma of what had happened in the bunker when his friend died. Suddenly, in the middle of what he was saying about the other man's courage and loyalty, my client found himself admitting something about his own actions "which I never speak about, even to myself." Informed of the presence of the enemy, he kicked open the door of the village shop, spraying the interior with bullets. There were no soldiers, only some women hiding there. He had killed two of them. "It was a mistake," he told me. "But that's no excuse."

They were real women and he had killed them. Excuses were irrelevant; he no longer lived in the world where excuses counted. These deaths cancelled the criteria which had shaped the world as recognisably the one where he lived. It all seems a sham now, he said. He said it angrily, remembering the way death had been sold him by the people who trained him, who had really seemed to believe the things they said: "Kill or be killed."

Courage and strength of character are not always what they appear to be – or what we would like them to be. We are all less tough than we think we are; indeed the process of thinking itself provides us with a way of not knowing our vulnerability, not really engaging with our fear. There is a close connection between the symptomatology of PTSD (post-traumatic stress disorder) and the experience of 'not thinking'; because we find ourselves suddenly deprived of our automatic ways of perceiving the situations in which we find ourselves, and neither 'fight' nor 'flight' is an available option, we automatically react by not thinking at all – which is why, instead of a memory we have an empty space, a blank. When memory returns it is in the form of terrifying 'flash-backs' as the thing we have avoided catches up with us. (This, of course, is what my client said so many times – "It has finally caught up with me at last, as I knew it would do.")

There is more here than a neurological reaction, or even a psychopathological defence mechanism, for that matter. The defensiveness is characteristic of the human species. We who fear pain, also fear its absence, which we immediately associate with death – with not being alive at all. Whether or not this occurs unconsciously, as Otto Rank claimed, it certainly characterises consciousness, as the history of civilisations clearly shows. My client assured me that he had never been afraid of dying; never particularly thought about it, in fact, even during his army training. The culture which trained him and made good use of his lack of thought, certainly did.

Not of its own death, however, but of its rivals, seeking to preserve its own life by destroying the lives of those perceived as threatening. The dominant urge within human societies has been to destroy rather than be destroyed, as fear expresses itself in the form of defensive aggression. Much has been written about the denial of death, but it is not denial so much as displacement – dying has always been an issue for human beings but societies protect themselves from taking it too personally by dwelling on someone else's death, not my own (my own being avoided by someone else's).

By now it should be obvious that this chapter is about human vulnerability and the defensiveness it gives rise to. Much of our public courage is of the corporate institutionalised sort, what Tillich described as the "courage to be as a part" (1962). This gives rise to a genuine feeling of belonging together and makes us feel considerably less exposed and conscious of our own weakness. The awareness of so many others in the same position as we feel ourselves to be, reassures us by lessening our individual loneliness, and we depend on it for a good deal of emotional support, as friendship groups, clubs and associations, separate nations and ethnic groups, and, of course, religions and philosophies. These, too, are the expressions of loneliness, and only manage to counter it by bringing its presence to the surface of life, so that it is all the more difficult to ignore. All are symbolic of a loneliness on which being human depends for its existence, the soul's gesture of incompleteness, the life which, in order to go on living, must give itself away. This is the individual soul's constitutive gesture, an exchange of voyages away from loneliness. Its action does not appear to be quantitative. A person who dare not undertake it will bring it into existence as a dialogue between separable parts of his or her own mind, as Melanie Klein and the Object Relations Psychotherapists established (Greenberg & Mitchell, 1983:119-150); many become conscious of it symbolised as a cause or an allegiance 'binding them together'. It is the wholeheartedness of the gift which counts rather than its scope. Indeed it must be so because the heart of the gesture is the irreducible action of loving-being-loved.

This being so, ways of approaching courage/defensiveness so that it can be brought to the surface in human relationship are bound to be qualitative not quantitative. These only need to two people on the pastoral care island. Indeed Holy Spirit may require only one person's presence at this time of discovery and psychic testing. The danger of large groups is that their enthusiasm is so easily misapplied, so that defensiveness shuns vulnerability altogether and erupts as violent aggression. Aggression of this public kind is easier to own, and to cope with emotionally, than the extremes of public defensiveness. My client's sorrow over his dead comrade only really achieves acknowledgement, could only really be felt in its full force, when the condoned aggression of war had disastrously backfired in the way he described. One way or another, officially or privately, our defensiveness hides itself away as excusable, heroic anger or private denial.

The defensive-aggressive reaction to psychological distress makes it hard for us to both give and accept the love we need as interdependent beings. Persons live within the dyad of self and other, which means that caring for other involves their care for us and also their willingness to be cared for by us. Pastoral care, as the expression of the Law of Christ, must be both received and given; it is a relationship not a commodity, which means that although it may involve elements which are quantifiable – more or less psychological understanding and organisational expertise – such things must never be allowed to assume control over a conscious awareness of my need to accept another's vulnerability and neediness as my own. What a Christian carer cannot or should not accept is the proposition that social roles are definitive of personal being, a thing we naturally do on the principle that vulnerability is always simply there to be overcome, at least so far as we are concerned, and the most effective way of doing this is by finding ways of perpetuating it in other people. From this point of view, then, social systems are devices for the control of human vulnerability by passing it on down the line, dealing with it simply by getting rid of it in an organised way, as if it were an unfortunate tendency which superior people must learn to overcome. These superior people are characterised as those who have found ways of off-loading their vulnerability by increasing that of their potential rivals – becoming better educated, earning more money, gaining more skill (one might also say living in the right part of the world, having better parents – or just being luckier!).

This, of course, is vulnerability used for aggressive needs which have the effect of turning it in on itself by its refusal to discern its true purpose, which is to bring home the awareness of a need which must be shared, not to distract us with the false hope that we can, in and for ourselves, guard ourselves against it through the acquisition of skills which set us apart from, rather than against, one another. Tillich defines faith as "accepting, acceptance because we are unacceptable" (1962); if we were acceptable – whole, complete, strong enough to cope with life and death – we would have no place in our universe for God's gift of unquestioning, creative love. This is the purpose and justification of our vulnerability, to lead us to a source of wholeness, to the acceptance of what we ourselves, in our individual identities, have never earned.

However skilful a practitioner may be, his or her true expertise will lie in a dependency taught by love. In practical terms this means that pastoral carers need to rely on their belief in and experience of mutual dependency, the acknowledgement of a vulnerability which alone can make their presence to the client a source of reassurance rather than criticism. If vulnerability is genuinely shared it works against the condescension which characterises even the most sensitive, well-meaning expertise in a hierarchically divided and divisive culture such as our own. Christ's mission subsisted in the removal of barriers we erect against one another, and it is these preoccupying assumptions about human superiority and inferiority which distract us from our true wholeness, which is to be found in weakness rather than strength. This is a gospel which may guide our pastoral care in even the most clinical of settings – perhaps even more here than anywhere else, in fact

There are some situations in which not depending entirely upon professionalism and technical skill may itself constitute therapeutic expertise. Surprisingly enough this can happen in the most unexpected places. Surgeons, even more than physicians, are generally considered to be very highly skilled indeed and it seems to be automatically assumed that their attitude to their patients will be particularly impersonal and probably highly technical: surely nobody can be afford to think of the body they are operating on as a living, breathing person! It seems much more likely that one can only do the job effectively by putting such thoughts entirely out of one's mind and concentrate on the matter in hand, dealing with it as simply as that – as matter, in fact. Such an attitude is in line with received wisdom with regard to the proper way to deal with patients of any kind, that the most dangerous thing professionals can possibly do is allow themselves to get personally involved with their patients. The surgeons I have spoken to, however, pay considerably more attention to their patients than physicians seem to do. When I asked them about this, they said that for them, the identity of their patients was something that they found themselves paying a lot of attention to precisely because they need to approach them as people and not as technical problems. Because the job they were doing required so much concentration upon the organic reality of the proceedings, because it could only be carried out by anaesthetising the individual concerned, so that any conscious personal relationship was cancelled out during the operation, the need for some personal contact before and after was more pressing. For the surgeon it was very important indeed that it was people

– a person – rather than a thing he or she was operating on, in order to preserve the heart of the healing transaction.

Obviously it is considerably easier to refuse to get involved. If it involves the gift of self to other in circumstances giving rise to the possibility of anxiety, then refusing to do this will almost certainly seem the safer option in case you listen too carefully to the patient and not closely enough to yourself – in which case you may run the risk of ending up making a mess of things. It is much easier to follow bad advice, particularly in the case of problems or difficulties of an emotional kind. Psychiatric conditions in particular are characterised by absence of judgement on the patient's part which means that only too easily professional helpers fall into the trap of never believing what they are told by a patient who sees things entirely differently from the way in which they do, and who, because of their illness, may very well be wrong. It is much more sensible to remain professionally cautious and be extremely wary of believing patients simply because they are certain they are right about things. (I clearly remember being told by staff members at the hospital where I worked that such and such a long stay patient must not be believed because she was a patient: "And she must be here for something, mustn't she, dear.")

These are examples of the courage necessary for taking chances not with people but for them; allowing them to be people rather than medical procedures. There is a real connection between our willingness to become involved with others to the point of uncertainty instead of taking refuge in the certainty of always being 'on the safe side' and so taking refuge in the thoughtlessness of certainty – or what seemed at the time to be certainty. I realise, of course, that there are very many kinds of physical procedures which have always to be carried out, and that unnecessary danger has to be avoided; all the same healing itself is never really automatic or technical; it is never something which people can simply do without any thought, because it is the intentional showing forth of care. This is why people do it, to show care, as a communication of concern; it is also why other people put themselves in someone else's hands without being a friend or a family member. Looked at like this, the technical aspect of medicine and its fellow healing disciplines falls into proportion, as a sophisticated extension of a healing gesture which in itself is indivisible, a single fact which hides its true nature behind a host of specialised expressions which have the effect of blurring its outline, making it seem less personal, less committed than it actually is.

An approach to healing which does not necessitate more equipment than empathy, patience and imagination depends all the same upon the way these ordinary human qualities are to be used. This kind of therapeutic equipment is applied directly by means of the carers themselves rather than the tools with which they have equipped themselves. In fact the pastoral care workers' main tool is seen to be their personal presence as this is experienced in the way they engage with someone else, in this case ourselves.

This is not as simple as it sounds. There is something else involved in our personal encounters with those in distress than imagination and a desire to make contact with someone else's pain. There is our own attitude towards the value of persons themselves. It is possible, for example, to approach individuals with empathy and insight while still regarding human beings themselves as less than personal; as a particular kind of organism which responds to this kind of treatment as other organisms do to more objective approaches. Like other 'tools of the trade' the approach via relationship may be employed for ends which are impersonal, if the philosophy directing it is itself basically impersonal. One may possess knowledge of and insight into human ways of reacting in order to discount it by subsuming all human phenomena under the overall heading of 'things which are potentially explicable in a scientific sense' – sophisticated and developed beyond any other objects of study, but objects all the same.

Christian faith invokes a source of strength, unity and healing which is "beyond measure"; and for pastoral care to be genuinely personal it must run counter to the dominant cultural assumption that the only therapeutic procedures which may be treated seriously are those seen to be scientifically validated, an attitude of mind to which we cling so defensively despite an overpowering amount of evidence to the contrary – an island of cognition in a sea whose width and depth are beyond measure.

The kind of knowing which restricts itself on purpose is the most effective way of preserving the status quo among and within human beings. When it comes down to it, this is a fundamentally manipulative knowledge, so that the beleaguered island, shut in by its own self-protective fear, stands for the strength which is really weakness – as Prospero realises when he abandons his magic and sets out again to sea, this time heading for home.

EPILOGUE

Prospero has his own agenda for his island. He has contrived it for a special purpose, and this is what it does. This being the case there are bound to be shortcomings in the attempt to cast it as all islands. To put this in another way, not every story will be the one embedded in the plot of this particular drama except insofar that, to be a story at all it must have a beginning, a middle and an end, and lend itself to the kind of focused meaning which fits the island-image so well. Just as islands begin and end with sea whichever way they are approached, so the things which they contain receive a kind of unity, a wholeness which comes from being circumscribed – this is the unity bestowed by location, being a place having an outline.

It is because of this speciality that islands lend themselves so well to story and storytelling. The island forms its contents into at least the possibility for story; because of its ability to detach itself from unfinished narratives about place and time which characterise our ongoing experience of life. Story will give a time we can hold on to and the island a definite place in which to hold on to it. An island, a story about what happened – is happening, will happen – there. Together they constitute two more or less fixed points within an ocean of possibility. There are all kinds of islands and all kinds of story; the only constant is the identity of both story and island as contained contrast – contrast made important by containment, shape given meaning by contingency, the coming together of change and certainty: once upon a time, there was an island ...

Story itself gives a significance to events by ordering them in terms of human problem solving and making sure that the necessary solution arrives when least likely, and from the most unexpected direction so that the denouement will constitute a satisfactory ending. An island setting concentrates our attention upon this problem rather than any other. What the problem actually is and where it manifests itself is not specified, or not in advance; in its pre-story, pre-setting state it can be anything at all. The possibilities of content – i.e. problematic situation – are as wide as the human imagination.

What is certain, however, is that they will not all concern stories, or islands, like Prospero's. Seen from this point of view, Prospero's island is an example of how events may become stories and islands be used as settings for stories. This is a particularly, even an outstandingly potent island, considering the effect it has on the people shipwrecked on it; all the same, some of the ideas about the significance of islands have been drawn from other places too, some of them real, some fictional, some a mixture of both, drawing on the imagery available to human beings whether or not they have actually lived on an island themselves, or even visited one. Islands possess an ability to fascinate, to take our imagination on a voyage, which is why they figure so much in works of fiction, particularly plays. Barrie's once-popular Mary Rose is mainly remembered nowadays for being "the island which likes to be visited". They still do …

In this book we have 'visited the island' for a series of purposes, one of which being its eagerness to receive us, and to place itself at our convenience as a milieu for exploring the theme of caring by looking at it from various angles, mainly ones related to Prospero's place of refuge.

This means that many pastoral concerns have been ignored. For instance, there is not very much about death here. Not in a literal sense that is: nobody really dies in The Tempest (except in Ariel's song, and even that turns out to be a metaphor: Ferdinand's father is far from being changed into actual coral – quite the opposite in fact, as the purpose of the play is to humanise its characters, not fossilise them!). This is not surprising, however, considering the association of death with islands which themselves promise some kind of renewal of life, an idea which recurs in places as widely separated from each other as Russia and Oceania (Grainger 1998). Perhaps the most famous description of it is in Malinowski's essay Baloma: the Spirits of the Dead in the Trobriand Islands.

> The *baloma* [soul] leaves the body immediately after death
> has occurred and goes to *Tuma* … *Tuma* is an island; one
> must therefore sail to it in a canoe!

Once having arrived on the island,

> the spirit settles down to a happy existence in Tuma, where
> he spends another lifetime until he dies again. But this new
> death is again not complete annihilation. (1974:160)

Isles of the dead tend to be stages within a process leading to a purer, higher existence. Such is the religious understanding; and it suggests another theme for *Prospero's Island*, that of 'the island as stepping stone'. The view of death presented here is a hopeful one; and this is the view implied by the play, too. In *The Tempest*, as Sandra Clark says, "vitality overcomes spiritual desolation" (1988:8). She goes on to point out that it is tempting to interpret Shakespeare's last plays as "versions of the myth of resurrection".

For Christians this is a temptation too powerful to resist; and there is certainly no reason why they should think of doing so. Quite the contrary: The Tempest in particular is a play which expresses Christian hope in an extremely powerful way, using the well-tried and perfectly accredited method of parable to do so. Those who themselves have been brought face to face with the reality of death have found drama a safe way of acknowledging their own distress (Grainger 2006). From time to time in this book I have drawn attention to the fact that human beings are physically and mentally vulnerable. There would be no need for pastoral care if this were not the case. When we are honest about ourselves we are willing to admit that we do in fact fear death; that we prefer not to think about it in a personal way, as applying to ourselves that is. Like other creatures, human beings fear the unknown, and our ability to imagine things not present makes it even harder to deal with. For us the solution is either some form of religious or spiritual hope for survival, or finding a way of controlling our thoughts in order to keep off the subject altogether.

Unfortunately the last method tends not to work very well. In an investigation into 'pathological grieving' which I carried out during my time as a hospital chaplain I became aware that

> there is considerable evidence that the refusal to
> acknowledge the event of death can have serious effects
> of a medical nature. There is reasonable agreement in the
> medical literature that sooner or later the death of a loved
> person must be acknowledged not only in theory but in
> fact, as something that has to be lived. The purpose of the
> process of grieving is to incorporate the fact of grieving

within the ongoing living awareness of the bereaved person. (1988:124, 125)

Inability to grieve and fear of death go together; and fear of death characterises our lives as individuals and societies. Inspired by Otto Rank, Ernest Becker tells us that it "makes wonderfully clear and intelligible human actions that we have observed with endless back and forth arguments about the 'true' human motives." (1973:*x, xi*)

Even the pre-occupation with sexuality owes its origin to the need to assert our conquest of our own limitations as creatures.

If the private, individual answer to the problem lies in denial and 'the displacement of anxiety' the public one has been dramatic, involving ritual and the corporate expression of human solidarity. This is the point made very forcibly by Malinowski, who maintained that the function of religion itself is "to set its stamp on the culturally valuable attitude; from this classically sociological angle the funeral ritual is the source of, and reason for, the beliefs it expresses" (1974:65).

The debate as to whether worship pre-dates religious systems is, of course, still an open question. The fact remains, however, that for many within our own society funerals mark two frontiers – that between an individual's life and his or her death, and that between the human race's belief in divine victory over death and our society's rejection, either explicit or implicit, of official institutionalised religion. This makes them very important indeed, for whatever they say they obviously assert something which people feel should be asserted – and are still the most firmly established way of doing this. Nowadays, why people go to other people's funerals is a matter which is very much up to them, but go they still do (Walter 1990; Grainger 1988, 1998).

As with funerals, so with other rites of a nature which is both corporate and highly personal. The action of corporate ritual embraces our awareness of death in a way and at a level which we find ourselves able to tolerate. In doing so, it transforms it into a shared reality. Like drama it calls on imagination to do this, as a dimension of human experience capable of involving us at a distance, which gives us the courage to involve ourselves. And this needs courage, for the prospect of contemplating death is itself, for us, a kind of dying.

This is precisely the kind of dying for which rites of passage exist. We can now see why Malinowski associates ritual with courage. At its heart the rite is intenselypersonal. Every life story is, and must be authentically their own, the result of their own experiences and the way that they themselves have interpreted the situations in which they found themselves: different experiences, different assumptions, different people. In funeral rites throughout the world this fact is given a particular dignity and importance, as each individual's personal story is viewed in the light of a wider narrative and draws a more profound significance from this. The result is that funerals everywhere possess a unity of intention expressed in the ritual process of "moving into higher ground" (Turner 1974; Grainger 1988). This is all the more personal for being a social commitment. As Eliade demonstrates so vividly, corporate rituals use the living and dying of individuals to reassure communities of a history and destiny, a past and future, which is genuinely shared; an account given of themselves and their transtemporal identity which can give meaning to the present and hope for what is to come .

Funerals, like other passage rites, are both typical and unique, individual and shared. Taking place against a sacred background they focus on an individual existence which is highly differentiated; personal, in fact. The purpose of these rituals is in fact initiation into a more authentic personhood, one which transcends difference in a new way of belonging together. They are individual as well as communal, as their underlying aim is the healing of social divisions, those between as well as within societies all because their origin lies in a deep respect for the significance of personal stories.

Because of this they are appropriate for the Epilogue to a book about islands. But islands and island places – hospitals, care homes, prisons and detention centres, residential and day schools, university campuses – all contain separate communities whose members reach out for a wider belonging which is able to undergird the security provided by their group identity.

Wherever passage rituals are performed they remain a celebration of life at its most personal level. Like islands, they concentrate and focus human existence. The memory of funerals which took place in a psychiatric hospital – another kind of island – stays with me:

> When somebody dies whose relatives cannot be traced
> and a few neighbours turn out to say goodbye to the old
> fellow whom they had never really liked very much anyway;
> when the number of patients in the female psychogeriatric
> ward at the mental hospital is reduced by the death of one
> isolated old woman, and the sister in charge brings along
> half a dozen patients, all equally old, equally isolated, to pay

their last respects "because she hasn't anybody, you now"; these are times when the funeral really counts, because this is what funerals are really about. On these occasions it is neither an individual nor a community that is bereaved, but humanity. And then Donne's famous sermon is revealed as simple existential fact rather than superb rhetoric: "Any man's death diminishes me because I am involved in mankind. And therefore never send to know for whom the bell tolls: it tolls for thee." (Grainger 1988:122-3)

It is not only entire lives which deserve to be laid to rest with due ceremony, however; the same holds true for important stages within our lives. At the end of The Tempest, in Act V Prospero quits his island and his own role as metteur-en-scène for those who for a short time have been his cast of characters. He does it ceremoniously with a dramatic "post-liminal" ritual, which he leaves us to imagine for ourselves so we may carry it away as a potent memorial of a task properly performed:

… this rough magic
I here abjure, and when I have requir'd
Some heavenly music – which even now I do –
I'll break my staff,
Bury it certain fathoms in the earth,
And deeper than ever did plummet sound
I'll drown my book. (Act V sc.1)

BIBLIOGRAPHY

Abrams B.A., Hogg   *The Social Psychology of Inclusion & Exclusion.*
M.A & Marques J.M.   New York: Psychology Press
(eds) (2000)

Aldridge (1996)   *Music Therapy: Research and Practice in
                        Medicine.* London: Kingsley

Anderson-Warren M   *The Shield of Perseus: Practical Approaches to
& Grainger R. (2000)   Dramatherapy.* London: Kingsley

Bailey E. (2001)   *The Secular Faith Controversy,* London:
                        Continuum

Bakhtin M.M. (1981)   *The Dialogic Imagination,* Austin: University
                        of Texas Press

Baxter E. (2007)   'Beloved Community: A Glimpse into the
                        Life of Holy Rood House' in J Baxter, (ed)
                        Wounds that Heal. London: SPCK

Becker E. (1973)   *The Denial of Death,* New York: The Free
                        Press

Berger P.L. &   *The Social Construction of Reality.*
Luckman T. (1967)   Harmondsworth: Penguin

Bion E.R. (1961)   *Experiences in Groups.* London: Routledge

Bowlby J. (1980)   *Attachment and Loss.* (3 Vols.) London: Hogarth Press and Institute of Psychoanalysis.

Brecht B. (1964)   *Brecht in Theatre* (trans J. Willett) London: Methuen

Buber M. (1961)   *Between Man and Man.* London: Collins

Buber M. (1966)   *I and Thou,* Edinburgh: T & T Clark

Campbell A.V. (1979   'The Politics of Pastoral Care', in D. Willows and J. Swinton, *Spiritual Dimensions of Pastoral Care.* Kingsley, 2000, p. 167

Cattenach A. (1992)   *Play Therapy with Abused Children,* London: Kingsley

Cattenach A. (1994)   'The Developmental Model of Dramatherapy' in S. Jennings, A. Cattenach, S. Mitchell, A. Chesner & B. Meldrum, *The Handbook of Dramatherapy,* London: Routledge, 1994

Clark S. (1988)   *The Tempest,* Harmondsworth, Penguin

Cooper A. (1997)   *Sacred Mountains,* Edinburgh: Floris

Crites S. (1986)   'Storytime: Recollecting the Past and Projecting the Future' in T.R. Sarbin, (ed.) *Narrative Psychology,* New York: Praeger

Duggan M. &   *Imagination, Identification & Catharsis in* Grainger R (1997)   *Theatre and Therapy,* London: Kingsley

Durkheim E. (1953)   *Sociology and Philosophy,* New York: Free Press

Durkheim E. (1970)   *Suicide: A Study in Sociology,* London: Routledge & Regan Paul

Erikson E. (1985)   *The Life-Cycle Completed,* New York: Norton

Fletcher S. & Jopling *Harrap's Book of 1000 Plays*. London: Harrap
N. (ed) (1989)

Foulkes S.H. & *Group Phychotherapy*. Harmondsworth:
Anthony (1957) Penguin

Frankl V. (1973) *Psychotherapy and Existentialism.*
Harmondsworth: Penguin

Freud S. (1917) 'Mourning and Melancholia' in *Collected
Papers* (1959) New York: Basic Books

Freud S. (1949) *An Outline of Psychoanalysis*. London:
Hogarth Press & Institute of Psychoanalysis

Frye Northrop. (1957) *Anatomy of Criticism*. Princeton: Princeton
University Press

Gennep A van. *The Rites of Passage*. London: Routledge and
(1960) Kegan Paul

Gersie A. (1987) 'Dramatherapy and Play' in S. Jennings (ed)
Dramatherapy Theory and Practice I. London:
Kingsley

Goffman E. (1968) *Stigma, Notes on the Management of Spoiled
Identity*. Harmondsworth: Penguin

Grainger R. (1988) *The Unburied*. Worthing: Churchman

Grainger R. (1998) *The Social Symbolism of Grief and Mourning*.
London: Kingsley

Grainger R. (1990) *Drama and Healing. The Roots of
Dramatheraoy*, London: Kingsley

Grainger R. (1992) 'Dramatherapy and Thought Disorder', in
S. Jennings (ed) *Dramatherapy: Theory and
Practice*, Vol 2, London: Routledge

Grainger R. (1995) *The Glass of Heaven, The Faith of the
Dramatherapist*, London: Kingsley

Grainger R. (1998) *The Social Symbolism of Grief and Mourning,*
London: Kingsley

Grainger R. (2002) *The Beckoning Bible.* Peterborough:
Methodist Publishing House

Grainger R. (2003) *Group Spirituality.* Hove: Brunner-Routledge

Grainger R. (2006) *Healing Theatre: How Plays Change Lives.*
Victoria B.C: Trafford

Greenberg J.R. & *Object Relations in Psychoanalytic Theory.*
Mitchell S.A. (1983) Cambridge, Mass.: Harvard University Press.

Gressvogel D.(1962) *The Blasphemers.* Ithaca NY: Cornell
University Press

Gunn G.B. (ed1971) *Literature and Religion.* London: S.C.M.
Press

Halmos P. (1965) *The Faith of the Counsellors.* London:
Constable

Hobson R. (1985) *Forms of Feeling: The Heart of Psychotherapy.*
London: Routledge & Kegan Paul

Hogg M.A. Fielding 'Fringe Dwellers: Processes of Deviance and
K.S. & Darley J. Marginalization in Groups' in D.A. Abrams,
(2005) M.A. Hogg & M. Marques, op.cit.

James W. (1902) *The Varieties of Religious Experience.* London:
Longmans.Green

Jones P. (2007) *Drama as Therapy:* London: Routledge

Jung C.G. (1963) *Mysterium Conjunctionis.* Collected Works,
vol 14. London: Routledge & Kegan Paul

Jung C.G. (1972) *Four Archetypes.* London: Routledge

Kastenbaum P. (1969) 'Psychological Death' in L. Pearson (ed)
Death and Dying. Cleveland, Ohio: Case
Western reserve University Press

Kelly, G.A. (1991)   *The Psychology of Personal Constructs.* London: Routledge

Lacan J. (1979)   *The Four Fundamental Concepts of Psychoanalysis.* Harmondsworth: Penguin

Lake F. (1966)   *Clinical Theology.* London: Darton, Longman and Todd

Lake F. (1980)   'The Theology of Pastoral Counselling', in *Contact,* 3.

Lake F. (1986)   'The Dynamic Cycle – Introduction to the Model, - *Lingdale Papers* 2, Oxford: Clinical Theology Association

Lambourne R.A. (1966)   'Treasure in a Large Earthen Vessel', *New Christian* Dec.15, p.17 (Review of F. Lake, *Clinical Theology.* 1966)

Landy R. (1994)   *Persona and Performance.* London: Kingsley

Langley D. (2008)   *An Introduction to Dramatherapy.* London: Sage

Lartey E. (2006)   *Pastoral Theology in an Intercultural World.* Peterborough; Epworth

Levinas E. (1987)   *Time and the Other* (trans. A Cohen) Pittsburgh. Pittsburgh University Press

Lidz T. (1983)   *The Person.* New York: Basic Books

Malinouski B.(1974)   *Magic, Science and Religion.* London: Souvenir Press

Major B. & Eccleston C.P. (2005)   'Stigma and Social Exclusion' in D.A. Abrams, M.A. Hogg, & J.M. Marques (eds) *The Social Psychology of Inclusion and Exclusion.* New York: Psychology Press

Marcel G. (1967)   *Searchings.* New York: Newman Press

Marcel G. (1984)

The Mystery of Being, Vol.I: Reflection and Mystery. Langham: University Press of America

Merleau-Ponty M. (1962)

Phenomenology of Perception. (trans. C. Smith) London: Routledge

New C. (2009)

'The "Sin" of Wal-Mart Architecture: A Visual Theology Reflecting Economic Realities', *Implicit Religion*, 12,1,21-50

Ojara P. (2006)

Toward a Fuller Human Identity. Bern: Peter Lang

Pargament K.I. (2007)

Spiritually Integrated Psychotherapy. New York: Guilford

Pearson C. (1944)

The Hero Within. San Francisco: Harper & Row

Perls F.S. Hefferline, R.F. & Goodman P.

Gestalt Therapy. Harmondsworth: Penguin

Pitruzzella S. (2009)

The Mysterious Guest. Bloomington, IN; i University

Poggi G. (1992)

Images of Society. Stanford C.A: Stanford University Press

Rogers C. (1967)

'The Process of the Basic Encounter Group' in J.F.T. Bugenthal, *Challenges of Humanistic Psychology.* New York: McGraw Hall

Rogers C. (1951)

Client Centred Therapy. London: Constable

Strawbridge S and Wolfe R. (2003)

'Counselling Psychology in Context' in R. Woolfe, W.Dryden, S.Strawbridge, *Handbook of Counselling Psychology.* London: Sage

Thoreau H.D. (1854)

Walden, in Baym N,et al., *The Norton Anthology of American Literature,* New York: Norton 1979

Tillich P. (1967)   *'My Search for Absolutes'*. New York: Simon & Schuster

Tillich P. (1962)   *The Courage to Be*. London: Collins

Twenge J.M. & Baumeister R.F. (2005)   'Social Exclusion Increases Aggression and Self-Defeating Behaviour while Reducing Intelligent Thought and Prosocial Behaviour', in D.A. Abrams, M.A. Hogg & J.M. Marques (eds) *The Social Psychology of Inclusion and Exclusion*. New York: Psychology Press.

Turner V. (1974)   *The Ritual Process*. Harmondsworth: Penguin

Walter T. (1990)   *Funerals: And How to Improve Them*. London: Hodder & Stoughton

Watts A. (1976)   *The Wisdom of Insecurity*. London: Rider

Weber M. (1930)   *The Protestant Ethic and the Spirit of Capitalism*. London: Allen & Unwin

Williams C. (1937)   *Descent into Hell*. London: Faber & Faber

Willows D. and Swinton J. (2000)   'Telling Tales' (with G. Lynch) in *Spiritual Dimensions of Pastoral Care*. London: Kingsley

Wilshire B. (1982)   *Role Playing and Identity*. Bloomington Indiana University Press

Winnicott D. (1971)   *Playing and Reality*. London: Tavistock

Winnicott D. (1980)   *The Piggle*. Harmondsworth: Penguin

Wright F. (1980)   *The Pastoral Nature of the Ministry*. London: S.C.M. Press

Index

147

F

Families 86, 115
Fiction 17, 21, 134
Flexibility 19
Funerals 38, 39, 136, 137, 138

G

Games 54, 56, 57, 117, 118, 119
Gardens 78, 91
Grief 30, 36, 37, 53, 125
Groups 26, 40, 41, 45, 46, 47, 48, 49,
    50, 52, 55, 58, 59, 60, 62, 63,
    64, 73, 77, 85, 95, 99, 127

H

Healing 10, 11, 12, 19, 21, 28, 34, 35,
    36, 37, 40, 60, 79, 80, 81, 84,
    85, 86, 88, 92, 98, 102, 104,
    130, 131, 137
Holy Rood House 91, 92, 139
Homecoming 78
Hope, Christian 135
Hospitals 35, 137

I

Identification 140
Imagination 6, 19, 32, 56, 66, 68, 82,
    86, 90, 91, 94, 96, 106, 112,
    117, 119, 121, 131, 134, 136
Implicitness 3
Incarceration 35
Inclusion and Exclusion 143, 145
Initiation 43, 137
Insecurity 70
Involvement 3, 11, 20, 21, 22, 24, 26,
    28, 33, 37, 54, 55, 58, 66, 69,
    84, 87, 88, 94, 100, 104, 116
Islands ix, x, 1, 2, 4, 8, 10, 40, 49, 55,
    69, 104, 105, 112, 124, 133,
    134, 137
Isles of the dead 135
Isolation 34, 46

L

Landscape ix, 4, 5, 6, 66, 94
Leadership 48, 123
Life-crises 84
Liminality 43
Lindisfarne 54, 56
Listening 15, 22, 33, 59, 65
Love xiii, 9, 22, 25, 44, 84, 85, 100,
    101, 102, 103, 104, 106, 123,
    128, 129
LSD 81

M

Making Sense 17, 62, 73, 75, 100
Maps 68
Metaphor x, 10, 91, 92, 134
Mountains 5, 6, 123
Mystery 144

N

Neonates 96

O

Oceans 2
Original Sin 72, 80

P

Passage rites 137
Pastoral Care iii, ix, 91, 140, 145
Permission iv, 32, 67, 88, 106
Personal Construct 52
Plays x, 7, 16, 21, 24, 36, 49, 67, 78,
    134, 135
Power 4, 5, 8, 15, 18, 20, 31, 48, 49,
    50, 51, 53, 58, 69, 73, 77, 106,
    112, 121, 122, 125
Prison 13, 14, 106
Professionalism 33, 120, 129
Profit and Loss 110
Psychoanalysis 72, 73, 80, 124
Psychotherapy 11, 92, 141, 142, 144
P.T.S.D. 126